Outcast press

I0638917

Slut vOmit II

Cover design by: Cody Sexton of A Thin Slice of Anxiety/Anxiety Driven Graphics

Copyright © 2024 Outcast Press

www.Outcast-Press.com

(e-book) ASIN: B0DX8L7DBY

(print) ISBN: 978-1-960882-17-2

About us

Slut Vomit is inspired by an actual cam girl (Fansly, Premium Snapchat model, and the like) who goes by the same name. Known for her creative handles (SlxtVxmit, p$ych Ward $horty, Pixie Stickz, Drügstore Cowgirl), and alt fashion sense (colorful hair, stretched ears, various tattoos and piercings), she is a visual representation of what it means to be transgressive.

In this second installment of *Slut Vomit*, you'll find 20 stories that delve into the sex industry's irony. If you somehow couldn't tell by the title, these stories might offend. We won't be sanitizing any language or content because these realities exist for some even if they don't for you.

Outcast Press believes the best fun entails some seediness. We long for the scummy, sickly, sticky, and sexy. We want the puritans of every religion—piously, politically, or de facto—to fuck off. Playing it safe is for off the page. As we taglined last time, Life is often "degrading" in a way that has nothing to do with sex, and so candid literature is what we writ(h)e for.

These pieces of love, lust, and loathing embrace the necessity of some vice to experience life at its fullest. Here's to spitting up what's festering inside until you're so empty, you can restart. May you find catharsis in the fall, fractures, friends, fiends, financial challenges and familial changes to rebuild from the splatter.

Sebastian Vice   Paige Johnson
Founder   Editor-in-Chief

Outcast Press

Table of contents

RazOrblade Pussy

By Manny Torres

They were chugging PBR tallboys in Ghoulie's car when Zaven belched so hard, she vomited. Down her cleavage and into her belly button, but it didn't stain her low-cut blouse.

She was lucky that way.

They sat in a Toyota Tercel with pink rims, parked in the alleyway behind the strip. Ghoulie stared at Zaven in disbelief before bursting with laughter. "Bitch," Ghoulie said. "Open the fucking door. You're like the third person to puke in my car this week."

Zaven forced the door open and let go again right there on the cobblestone. She wiped, breathed, then puked again. "I can smell it," Zaven said. Her accent made it sound like *I caan smellit*.

"What?"

"All da puke on the cobblestone."

"Are you okay?"

Zaven wiped her mouth and nodded. "Empty stomach. I'm pure and cleaned out now."

"You imagine all the puke saturating these bricks?"

"That's why Tampa smells like piss and puke all da time. I just added to it. You're welcome."

"Yes!" Ghoulie high-fived her.

Zaven slammed the door shut and took a long, deep breath.

"I fucked Evan right there on the hood of his Camaro," Ghoulie said. "Jody, Clown, and Frankie watched."

"Is that when you did the movie?"

"No, da movie was after we broke up. We did it in da back of Frankie's pickup. Clown filmed it. Just Felicia and me. We popped a champagne bottle and took turns pouring bubbly over each other and then put the empty bottle in our pussies."

"Girl, that's not good. I'm not going to tell you what to do, but that's dangerous as fuck. That's how you really pop your coochie."

They finished the last can. Belched, snorted, laughed.

"Who's this you're hooking up with?" Ghoulie smacked her lips in her usual, classless way.

"Lamont and his creeps," Zaven said.

"You turning into their Avon lady."

"This is about getting my own block. My own girls."

"Nice. You with the Russians now?" Ghoulie asked.

"No. But I let them piss on me sometimes, so I have an in. Persians too. They're more into ass-kissing and feet. Right now, I gotta go in and play nice."

"What about the Haitians?"

Zaven stuck out her tongue in disgust. "I don't know who's worse."

"Aren't you Russian?"

"I'm Albanian," Zaven said. "I came to America on a Russian boat though."

Ghoulie giggled. "Your ass got trafficked into the States."

Zaven steamed for a moment. "Weren't you conceived at a family gathering?"

"Fuck you. Just 'cause I'm from Kentucky..."

"Don't matter."

"Bitch, you're the one with the weird eyes, like you're some dumpster butt baby. I can't tell if you're Mongolian or Eastern European."

They giggled themselves into silence.

Ghoulie burped. "Hmm. I wanna get fucked up, but I'm not sucking dick for drugs."

"Since when do you pass on a meat stick? Sometimes you gotta do what you gotta do." Zaven showed her the nickel-plated .357 2" in her small purse.

"You robbing him? It's domino night at the old stink hole. There'll be a lot of N-words there."

"A girl has to be persuasive," Zaven said. "I'm here to establish shit. They better recognize. This is just if the talks fail."

"They only wanna see your ass."

"They've all had a taste of it."

"Ew, they're all black."

"So?"

"So, they're big and black."

"Bitch, please," Zaven said. "I've sucked my way through da 36 Chambers of Dong, so it's nothing I haven't inhaled before."

"Huh," Ghoulie said. "Didn't Snapshot tell you to never do a gangbang?"

"He was an impotent, fat old man. He thought he owned me because he took pictures of me when I was 15."

"Is he in jail?"

"Worse: He moved to L.A."

"Aw. I've always wanted to go to L.A.," Ghoulie said.

"What's stopping you?"

Ghoulie shrugged.

"Anyway, it wasn't a gangbang," Zaven said. "Not that it matters. Do I look like I have any shame?"

"But they were gloryholes. That counts."

"No, it doesn't. It was a blowbang. Learn da difference."

"Guess I'll never go pro, like you."

Zaven nodded and impatiently sighed. "You in?"

"I wanna get fucked up, if that's what you're asking."

"Well, you need shit to get fucked up with. So, you holding anything?"

"Nothing, babe. I told you, I'm not sucking anybody's dick for drugs tonight."

"Never stopped you before," Zaven said. "Don't worry. You won't need to. I got this."

"Maybe I should stay in the car."

"Bitch."

"I don't have a gun!"

Zaven rolled her eyes and sprayed herself with cheap perfume. Her denim skirt was tight and short, barely covering the toe of her delta. She grabbed a fast-food napkin off the floormat and wiped between her cleavage and legs. She opened her pale legs and sprayed between them. "Haven't washed in a minute."

"Ew."

"Bitch, when's da last time *you* showered?" Zaven got out of the car, slamming the door. To avoid looking like a cheap hooker, Zaven wore denim and leather to blend in. The leather couture elevated her status. Better to look like a coke whore and recognized for her screenwork than a cheap Nebraska Ave. hooker. Her makeup was heavily applied but fabulous. Batwings on her eyelids, upward rouge strokes against her cheeks. "You better be here when I get back. Don't know how long I'll be."

"Long enough for you to suck 40 dicks."

"Fuck you. No. That's not going to happen. Be here and be ready. Shit might go down."

Ghoulie nodded, knowing full well that her car was about to die from various ailments but agreed anyway, watching Zaven walk off.

Zaven went up the alley that smelled of piss and vomit then turned left on 15th and headed toward 7th Ave., into the hullabaloo of Ybor City. The usual Saturday night dissonance lit up around her. Every weekend was Fat Tuesday. Cars drove past, floating on neon lights, blaring music, whistles, and catcalls too. Her middle finger stood long and high for all of them.

The old candle and hippie incense store had converted into a hookah bar. She stopped for a moment, lit up whatever was in her glass pipe until the rush got her going. She'd share a PBR with Ghoulie, but never her inhalant chemistry.

Ybor City was roasting tonight. Literally. Like, on the next block, Traxx was on fire. Flames flickered up and out over the sidewalk and into the sky with an apocalyptic bloom. She was afraid her fluffy hair would catch fire, so she followed a parade of goth kids marching in line at Club Inferno. She felt old, walking in the fold of these black-caped vampires in their cement-block platform boots, but they barely noticed her.

Already, the firetrucks were arriving and soon the street would clog. There'd be no way Ghoulie was going to drive a getaway car in this traffic. *Noted.*

Zaven crossed to the next block and, in a small alleyway beside the old botanica, was a hairy biker getting blown by somebody on their knees. She rolled her eyes.

Tampa, Florida, Zaven thought. *Anything goes.* Somewhere out there, was a tree with the inscription **Sodom Loves Gomorrah** carved into its trunk.

When she reached the club, there was a group of men at a small table, playing dominoes in the patio. They sucked hookah hoses, confabulating in whatever their language was. They were mostly Caribbean so theirs was a creole polyglot. Zaven didn't speak it but had been around enough of them to get the basics. Next to the club was a cigar bar, where Cubans in fedoras smoked with an established apartheid between them and the black islanders.

Dozens of eyes looked her over. The Cubans sucked their teeth, which was their cannibalistic reaction to a white woman. The blacks had spit-roast recollections of her.

The door man let her pass. She squeezed past him and let him feel her body close. She even gave him a smile for his trouble. Better he feels her soft curves than the gun in her bag. She ascended the iron stairs to the second floor, where the club overlooked the street.

Club Compas was on the second and third floor of a French Colonial building. At the landing, she made a right and was immediately in their presence. The balcony railing was wrought iron, like the ones in New Orleans. It was smoky up there, a strobe light throbbing in a corner. Another lamp in the opposite direction shot up beams of neon pink and teal. Ceiling fans twirled slowly. She stood at the entrance for a moment, hands at her hips. No one noticed. The music was low. Crowd noise from the street below. A fraudulent Mardi Gras pounded the night.

The gang, if you could call them that, hung loose. Dressed down: denim shorts and loose white T-shirts. At least the Cubans at the cigar bar wore guayaberas with their short pants and black leather sandals. This group was mostly black, mostly Haitian.

"Fuck," she said. "What kind of vibes you got going in this circle jerk?"

When the smoke cleared, or perhaps her vision, she saw the black woman sitting on a wicker chair in a corner. The woman liked to sit amongst her people, so there was no desk or big throne. The rest of her crew lounged on the long velvet couches, smoking giant blunts.

The woman stood up and walked toward Zaven, braids swishing down to her waist. Her nails were silver talons with diamonds at the tips. Her skin was pure chocolate, so she appeared naked in her tight brown leggings.

"Where's Lamont?" Zaven asked.

"Times are changin', so is the personnel," the woman told her. She turned to her crew. "Ha ha. She calls Lay-Lay, Lamont. Cute. His moms would be so proud."

"Who da fuck are you?"

"Call me Mighty Afrodeity, bitch." She did not have an island accent. "You must be the girl with the razorblade pussy. Lotta mufuckas gettin' they dicks cut, they go up in there. Things won't be like with Lay-Lay, ya dig?"

"I don't give a fuck who you are," Zaven said, hand on her hip—but her purse was close too. The .357.

The room paused to direct attention at them. Joints frozen in mid-air. Someone killed the music.

"This won't take long," said Zaven.

"Either getchoo a table or step the fuck out, hoe."

"I won't be bringing anymore of my girls in here no more, you hear? Any further business requests will be through me, at a location of my choosing. Okay? Lamont owed me money, so I'm here to collect."

With her outfit and hair, Afrodeity looked like a supervillain. "Nah, I seen the ledgers. Nobody owe you shit. I got dem receipts. You just tryna get that extended warranty? Yeah, we don't play that. And I'm afraid this new thing we got don't extend to used merchandise. And bitch, fuck if I care you ain't running tricks up in here. Them hoes is worn out—and so is you."

There was no god, no magic in the room. It was a black vortex, weighed down by the force of its own negative energy.

"This ain't *Soul Train* I'm running here," Afrodeity said. "You wanna pick something up, I might could accommodate you. But ain't gettin' nothing free."

"I'm here for what's due to me and then I'm out."

"Baby girl, whatever he owed you, that's between you and Lay-Lay. He ain't here no more, so take your mermaid ass someplace else."

Zaven knew not to probe where he was or where he was taken to. She said, "If you didn't know, sis, I did his books but, most important, brought in girls from my school. Young poosy. And they helped distribute too. Pass it around like candy."

"And?" Afrodeity stepped up. "You act like nobody ever done secretary work 'round here. Every one of these niggas up in here help me get the merch out. Ain't you got school tomorrow?"

"Without me, you think you can get the good poosy I brought in?"

"Bitch, we in Ybor City. I can traffic all the hoes of the world right up in here. I even got your girl tricking for me."

"Who da fuck you talking 'bout?" Zaven asked.

"That girl you fucked in the truck. I seen your movie."

"I'm a classy lady. I never fucked no girl on truck. You got me mixed up with someone else."

"Ion know," Afrodeity said. "Maybe. Y'all crackers look the same to me. Anyhow, that bitch was here 'fore you showed up. Same thing. Begging for scraps."

Afrodeity signaled for her henchmen to grab a girl from behind the bar. They brought out a malnourished girl, her Eurotrash outfit torn and soiled.

"Da fuck..." Zaven said. "The fuck you do to her?"

"Not us," Afrodeity said. "That's all her. She let them wear her out in exchange for getting dusted. I mean, she let them run a train and they gave her what she wanted. And what she wanted was to get dusted."

Zaven wanted to run. But that's not how you planted a flag and claimed territory.

"Go on, take her," Afrodeity said. "They done with her."

"She's not my friend."

Afrodeity sucked her teeth. "That's hella waste of a white girl."

"You can keep her. I ain't leaving without my money."

"You barking up the wrong leg, doggy. I ain't got your money."

"I give my soul to this place, I give time, and da girls. My own money. Lamont and I had a loan agreement. Cash or stash, bitch."

"Bitch, no," Afrodeity said. "You best get to stepping or it's gonna get wild up in here. And take that dusty ass bitch witchoo."

That was when Zaven pulled the .357 out of her purse.

"Listen..." Zaven stepped back. "Let's talk this out and settle it as quiet as we can."

Every person in the room, from players to the bartender to the crossdresser serving drinks, pulled their guns and aimed at Zaven.

She turned whiter than the girl beside her.

Afrodeity crossed her arms. "Nah, we ain't doing that. Put that away 'cause every nigga here is working for me."

Zaven knew when she was licked. All over.

Felicia grabbed her and pulled her through the doorway she'd entered. They took a left and tumbled down a short flight of steps. Wrought iron stairwell. Z-shaped. Upstairs led to the roof bar, down steps went into immediate darkness and a metal door on the ground floor. Sounded like the A/C unit was growling down there, along with an industrial water heater and vent. The pulse of machinery was deafening.

From the top of the stairs, Afrodeity's silhouette loomed.

Zaven scrambled and pushed through the metal basement door, shutting it behind them. She stuck her hand in her purse, but the gun was gone. "Fuck, it fell out," she said. "Should have hide it in my poosy."

The room was a storage closet repurposed into a lab. A kitchen. Tungsten lighting buzzed overhead, and it smelled of sweat and burning chemicals. Burning plastics. Zaven knew the smell. It was a miasma that occasionally filled her lungs from the bell-end of her glass pipe. There was a naked black man wearing goggles and safety covers over his Timberland boots.

"Welcome, ladies," the man said. "Looks like you have your work cut out for yourselves today." He dangled about 12" of licorice-colored penis in front of them. It made him look more alien with those goggles.

They stood in the corner as he strutted around the tight enclosure.

As he moved around, he kept singing, *"Two for the money"* from "Blue Suede Shoes." That's it. Just, *"Two for the money, two for the money,"* like a stuck record. Over and over, circling the kitchen island crowded with his makeshift chemistry set.

"He's okay," Felicia said. She eyed the beakers and tubes and bags. "We probably shouldn't be in here without a mask. For too long." Her eyes rolled into the back of her head. She had to lean on the walls to stay on her feet.

"You been living down here?" asked Zaven. She covered her mouth after inhaling. Immediately, the bell rang in her head. The 15-second high.

"For a minute. I do what they say, and they get my fix."

The man told them, "When I finish this bake, you bitches can help me box it up."

Zaven gave the room a look over, seeing discarded packs of cough medicine and household cleaning supplies. She wondered why Afrodeity wasn't pounding on the door. The music upstairs shut off, replaced by bursts of shouting in creole French and lots of furniture-throwing.

The man laughed. "Somebody lost a game."

"They get that way on Fridays," Felicia said.

The shouting was then replaced by gunshots.

The man looked down at them with bug eyes.

"You're da only one working here?" Zaven asked.

"This is my first week," he said. "You bitches ain't leavin' 'til we clear this shit out."

The sputtering of an Uzi and several gunshots sounded upstairs. Things got quiet before they erupted into screaming and more shooting.

Zaven saw the toolbox under the lab table and had two choices: the ball-peen hammer or the long Phillips-head screwdriver. Without further hesitation, she grabbed both.

"Shit," the impromptu scientist said. He boxed the first batch. He ran out of boxes when he tried to also store his chemicals and cheap mixing tools. He scrambled around and Zaven managed a chuckle, watching him flop around in a panic. He turned from packing and came at her angrily.

She stabbed his neck with the screwdriver and swung the hammer at his face.

He tumbled loudly and sloppily over the chemistry table and fell to the floor.

She saw the sawed-off pump shotgun propped against a chair near him and helped herself to it.

"What are we doing?" Felicia asked.

"We? I'm getting out of here," Zaven said. "Is there another exit?"

Felicia stumbled around, barely balancing on her dingy white heels. "Sure...under the stairs. Outside the lab."

"Help me open this."

They wedged a thin baking sheet into the slit of the door and pulled it open.

"Can I come too?" Felicia asked.

Zaven looked at her. "You can fuck off."

There was a war erupting on the upper floor. That was more of a Miami thing, but Tampa was acting like Tampa tonight.

"I'm coming with you!" Felicia crept up behind her.

"Bitch, you better find your own way," Zaven said.

"You're my bestie, girl. I ate your pussy that one time."

"That was acting," said Zaven. "That's what we do in the industry. You have some fucking guts to ask...after you sold me out. We were never friends, never will be. You're on your own. Go throw yourself at them. They'll take you back. Any white woman is a good woman."

Slowly, Zaven crept out of the lab, looking up at the stairwell. Sounded like a stampede of elephants at a Mexican standoff. She went for the exit.

Felicia was heading upstairs. "Hey," she shouted. "Down here! The lab's down here!"

"You fucking bitch," Zaven said, pushing through the door and right into the presence of two armed men.

These guys were not like the Haitians shooting it out upstairs. They aimed, and she quickly tossed the shotgun.

"Hey, I need a ride out of here," Zaven said to them.

Two men: dark, hairy Persian men armed with Desert Eagles. They looked her up and down from behind their sunglasses.

Zaven craned her head down the other side of the alley.

A circle of empty PBR cans where the car had been. Ghoulie and her pink rims were gone.

Zaven cursed her name under her breath and cursed her to be burned alive. In a few days, Zaven would return with her cousins: Dor, Teo, Erm, and the rest. They'd sweep through the remains of Club Compas with Uzis and shotguns and claim it. The bar, the dancefloor, the meth lab. The gunfight between the Persians and Haitians would slim the ranks on both sides, allowing Zaven to waltz in, poosy-first and take it over. Her reign would sweep from Tampa, all the way across the state to Odyssey.

But right now, she had to get past these two goons.

"Nobody leave premises," one of the men said. He was rolling a toothpick over his tongue, which reminded her of one of the hundreds of men she'd fucked in front of a camera.

"You that girl," the other Persian said. "How you get out of jail?"

Zaven gave him the look. The sharp, sleepy eyes that got her on the screen. Back when she was not of age, passing around several forged documents to get whatever she wanted. "Let's go," she said. "Behind that dumpster and I'll show you. Works every time."

Author Bio

Facebook: @MA Torres   Instagram: _M.A.Torres

Manny Torres is author of the Dead Dogs trilogy, dark crime-comedy novels that can be read as standalones. Most recently, that includes *Cabrones Perros*, where characters from this story feature. His stories, often dealing with Georgia and Florida lowlifes, also appear in *Starlite Pulp Review #3, #4, American Muse*, and he wrote the hilariously grisly intro to Craig Clevenger's *Diner Noir,* entitled "Get in, loser. We're Going to Waffle House!"

Torres also has a piece in *Bishop Rider Lives* and you can catch up on all his projects at www.MannyTorresNovelist.com

More From Our Authors

Noir

An Anthology
Curated by
Craig Clevenger

Boat Drinks

By John Kojak

Mark lived on a boat. A 38-foot Chris-Craft Commander he named the *Pura Vida*. But it wasn't the kind of motor yacht you see jetting across turquoise waters on the covers of magazines, or dockside at some fancy bayside seafood restaurant. Mark's boat was the type of floating fiberglass refuse you find tied up to the cheap slips in the back of the marina. The ones with leaky hulls and engine issues that looked like they would sink as soon as they left the dock. That kind.

Mark's boat wasn't going anywhere, but it didn't need to. *The Pura Vida* had a singular purpose: poontang. And it fulfilled its purpose well, I can attest to that. I didn't live on the boat with Mark, but I would come down on weekends during the summer. We would hit the beach during the day, then at night we would grab a few bottles of booze and some blow and prowl the seaside bars looking for young blonde cokeheads with daddy issues. It never took long. The promise of a few lines and boat drinks did it every time. It was good times, but nothing good last forever.

It was the weekend before Labor Day, and Mark and I were sitting out on the stern of his boat, drinking beers and talking about women—Mark loved to talk about women. He was halfway through a tale about his latest squeeze, a dancer from a local pole farm, when she came slithering up the dock in a skimpy tube-top, threadbare cutoffs, and high heels like a camel-toed Leviathan.

"Speak of the devil..." Mark said as he popped the top on a fresh can of beer. "Here comes Trinity right now."

I looked around the side of the boat. I wouldn't say she was hot, but she was young. And in the pussy game, young counted for a lot. "Trinity—is that her stage name?"

"Who cares." Mark grinned like a fox. "As long as I can tap that ass, she can call herself whatever she wants."

We were both doubled over laughing when she got to the back of the boat.

"Who's that?" Trinity asked as she waved one of her neon-pink, dagger-tip fingers at me.

"That's my boy, Danny," Mark said.

"He's cute..." she said as her eyes scanned my body for necklaces, watches, rings, or anything else of value. I got the feeling she was the type of girl who was more interested in the bulge of a man's wallet than the one in his crotch.

Trinity reached out to Mark for a helping hand as she awkwardly stepped on board in her clear plastic stilettos. She was something, I wasn't exactly sure what, but I could see why Mark liked her. She was just his type: young, dumb, and looking for fun. But whatever she lacked in years, she made up for in miles.

"You must be Trinity," I said as I put my hand around her waist and leaned in for a loose hug. Her bare flesh felt strangely mushy, like a wet sponge, and she smelled like a sickly-sweet combination of diesel fuel and cheap perfume. "Mark was just telling me about you."

She gave me a quick air-kiss on the cheek and turned to Mark. "I'm sorry I didn't call you, baby. Me and my momma got in a huge fight today." She flicked her cigarette into the water, then opened her purse to pull out another one. "I told her I had to dance tonight, and she started trippin'... Called me a bad mother and a crackhead and shit—so I just took off. I didn't really know where to go. I hope you don't mind me just showing up like this."

"Naw, baby. I understand." Mark wrapped his huge brown paws around her tight little white-girl ass and pulled her in close to his crotch. "You had to get some of this, didn't you?"

"Hell yeah, I did," she said before giving him a mouthful of sloppy tongue.

He had dipped his wick in worse—we both had. But she had **white trash trainwreck** written on her forehead in neon letters. This was going to be a shitshow, and I knew it was going to take more than a few beers to get through it. I went into the cabin and broke out the party supplies I had stashed in my backpack. I tapped out a few lines worth of crystal on the small glass stovetop and began to chop it down.

"After I left, that crazy bitch wouldn't stop calling and texting me—saying she was going to call the cops on me for abandoning my kids and shit," Trinity griped as she walked into the small galley. "The po-po won't be able to find me though... Check this out." Trinity unzipped her glittery purse and turned it upside down. A half-empty pack of Marlboro 100's, a small glass pipe, and the busted-up remains of a smartphone tumbled out onto the counter. The back of the phone was broken off and the battery had been ripped out.

"*Jezus*, why didn't you just turn the damn thing off?" I asked before bending down and snorting a long, fat line.

"That don't work... If you really don't want nobody to find you, you gotta bust it up," she said with the conviction of someone speaking from experience.

"Sounds like that could get expensive," I said, feeling the rush.

"I'll just get one of my customers to buy me another one." She fluttered her long, fake eyelashes at Mark and raked his chest with her razor-sharp nails.

"Pretty sure I got an old flip phone around here somewhere," Mark replied.

"*Um-huh. Broke ass...*" She made a flippant *tsk* with her tongue and glanced toward my pile of glistening white powder.

Mark was eyeing the candy too.

"Hook me up, homie," Mark said, crowding in next to us.

"Ladies first," Trinity said as she reached for a shiny metal straw on the counter.

"Bros before hoes." Mark shoved her aside like a bad bowl of clams and laid out a nice, thick line of crystal for himself. After he was done, he scraped what powder remained into a line for Trinity that was as thin and scraggly as she was.

She didn't complain though. I think she was used to getting the leftovers.

"It's hot..." She took her bump. "You got some drinks around here or what?"

"Of course." Mark reached into the cooler and pulled out an ice-cold can of beer.

"Yuck, I don't want beer... I want something sweet."

"You should've let me know you were coming. This is all we got," Mark said.

"I didn't know where I was gonna go, I just had to get the hell out of that house. Those damn kids was driving me crazy—I need to party."

"You can hang here, baby, but you need to hook up my boy." Mark nudged me with his elbow. He knew I needed to get some trim too. "Why don't you call your girl, Mercedes, and tell her to get that phat ass over here?"

"I can't call nobody—my phone's broken," Trinity hissed.

"Jesus Christ, you can use my phone," Mark growled back.

"That's not what I meant. I don't know anybody's number—they were all in my phone."

"Well, you better think of something, or you can carry your scrawny ass back home to your busted-out trailer."

"Don't start talking shit. I can replace your black ass—like that." She reached out and snapped her fingers in Mark's face.

Mark's hand shot out like a rattlesnake. It coiled so tightly around her throat, her eyes looked like they were going to jump out of her skull. "Bitch! Don't you ever talk to me like that," he seethed through clenched teeth.

I was shocked. I knew Mark had a short fuse, but I had never seen him put his hands on a woman. Not like that, anyway.

Trinity didn't say anything else. She just blankly stared back at him until he let her go. Then she calmly reached down and lit another cigarette. "I want a daiquiri—a strawberry daiquiri."

Mark's hands were shaking, and he had a look in his eyes I hadn't seen before.

I knew I had to get him out of there before he totally lost his shit. "Let's go to the liquor store, man. Get some real drinks," I said quickly.

Mark didn't move.

"C'mon, man, let's roll." I tried to pull him away from her, but he wouldn't budge.

Mark glared at Trinity for what seemed like an eternity before he finally followed me out.

We didn't talk until we pulled into the parking lot of the local Booze Mart. Mark still looked pissed as he slammed the car in park.

I tried to pull him back to his senses. "You giving that chick money or what?" I asked after he shut off the engine.

"Hell nah, there are plenty of suckers at the titty bar who do that."

"That's cool," I said. "But you know they ain't giving her cash and buying her phones and shit for nothing...right? So why are you trippin'?"

"I want her to know I ain't no punk, like those little bitches stuffing dollar bills in her panties, that's all."

"Hit it and quit it, son. You know the drill."

"Yeah, you're right." He let out a big, heavy breath. "Too many fishes in the sea..."

"Damn right." I gave him a knowing fist bump.

Mark seemed to calm down after that. We went inside the liquor store and loaded up on rum, vodka, tequila, and a gallon of strawberry daiquiri mix. We grabbed a large bag of ice on the way out and headed back to the boat.

The sun was hovering just above the horizon when we got back. The marina was starting to fill up with the typical weekend crowd: doctors, dentists, and douchebags who had big shiny sailboats that could actually go somewhere, but rarely did. Instead, they would bring their wives, mistresses, and Tinder dates out to their boats on the weekends to sip wine or piña coladas and watch the sun go down for the same reasons Mark and I did: to get laid.

When we walked inside, the cabin was empty. I sat the liquor on the counter next to the stove, and Mark threw the large bag of ice in the sink and began hacking away at it with the butt of a steak knife. When he was done, he threw a few big chunks into the blender, along with conspicuous amounts of rum and a little strawberry daiquiri mix for color—he had the routine down cold.

While Mark was making the drinks, I peeked through the hatch into the stateroom below, half-hoping/half-praying that Trinity had left, but there she was—splayed out on the bed like a garage-sale Barbie. I thought she was out cold, but as soon as she heard the blender, she popped up like a strung-out Jack-In-The-Box.

She bounded up the steps into the galley and softly kissed Mark on the neck. "Don't be mad, baby. You know I love you."

"Is he the one, Trinity?" I asked.

She didn't bother to look at me. I'm sure she had heard that line a thousand times before—but I thought it was funny.

Trinity pulled at her super tight tube-top. It looked like a rubber band stretched around an elephant. "My daughter needs to grow some tits, her cloths barely fit me."

"How old is your daughter?" I regretted asking as soon as the words fell out of my mouth.

"She's nine..."

Her daughter's life flashed by my crank-addled brain. In a few years, she would be the one swinging from poles and looking for boat drinks just like her mom. Tragic as it was, that was the type of women we preyed on.

Mark filled our plastic party cups with icy strawberry daiquiris, and we went outside to sit on the stern. I don't know if I could live on a boat, but you couldn't beat the sunsets. The sun was bobbing like a float on the water, and I was staring off toward the edges of the world, mesmerized as the crimson rays danced across the waves, when a friendly face poked its head up behind the boat.

It was a dolphin. I had seen them in the marina, but never this close. Mark saw it too.

"Hey, that's one of my buddies," he said with a big smile. "Guess they figured out that I'm always around, so they like to come by and say hi."

Trinity lit a joint—took a long, deep hit—and then asked, "Is that a shark? My son likes sharks... He's really dumb."

I shook my head and snatched the joint out of her hand. Her son was dumb? I don't think she realized how stupid *she* was.

"Watch this." Mark grabbed an orange life preserver off a hook next to the cabin door and flung it about 20 feet into the water.

It was like tossing a ball to a dog. The dolphin quickly swam after it, grabbed the ring in its mouth, and excitely swam back to the boat. Best part, it used its snout to fling the life preserver back up into Mark's hands. It was amazing. Mark and his little buddy played the game a couple more times before the dolphin finally got bored and swam off.

"That is cool as shit." I took a hit off the joint. It tasted like Mexican dirt weed.

"Yeah, those dolphins are smart as hell. They are always bringing stuff up to the boat—I need to train them to bring me some pussy."

I don't know if it was because we were so high, but we both laughed so hard, we almost pissed ourselves.

Trinity didn't look like she thought it was too funny though... "I didn't come here to play with fish," she said tersely. "You got any more Cristy?"

I thought about correcting her, but I was having too much fun. "Hell yeah, I do."

We all went back inside, and I tossed her the little bag of meth. "Help yourself." Those weren't words I usually said to strippers—especially when it came to drugs, but I was feeling generous.

Trinity was on it like white on rice. She cut up the crank and had it lined out quick as a cat.

"Where is that straw thingy?" she asked.

I saw the thin aluminum tube we had been using next to the blender. I picked it up and peered through it, into the light. It was as about as long and round as a soda straw, and I could see that the inside was coated in powdery residue. I figured that was why Mark wanted to use it, so there would always be a little bump in there when he needed it. "Do you got anything smaller, man?" I said to Mark as I handed the metal tube to Trinity.

"If you want something smaller, we can use Mark's dick," she said just before bending over to snort a line.

Mark's hand came down on her head like a hammer—*Bam!*

Trinity sprang straight up.

The tube was gone, it must have shot right up her nose! There was a little stream of blood flowing out of her right nostril.

She stood eerily still for a moment, then began stumbling around the cabin with her hands thrust in front of her like a doped-out zombie—until she tumbled down the steps, into the small stateroom below.

"What the hell, man? Are you fucking cray?" I couldn't believe what I'd just seen. I peered down the stairs.

Trinity was flopping around on the deck like a fish out of water.

"What did you do that for?"

"I'm sick of her shit..."

"That's just *great.*"

She stopped flopping.

"I think you fucking killed her."

Mark wasn't a saint, neither was I, but I never imagined he could just end somebody like that.

I rushed down the stairs to see if she was really dead. I pulled Trinity up by her shoulders and shook her hard. "Trinity! Trinity!" I looked for any sign of life, but her neck was swinging back and forth like a rubber chicken and her eyes were cold and dark as a dead fish. He fuckin' killed her...

It hit me like a giant wave.

I looked up at Mark.

His face showed no emotion at all. "What do you think we should do?" he casually asked.

What should WE do, motherfucker? I thought it, but I didn't say it. "Shit, man. I don't know..." I stood up and sat on the edge of the bed. I needed to think.

Mark was like a brother to me, so calling the police was out of the question. But helping him sounded even worse.

Mark must have seen the panic in my eyes. "She was just a whore, bro."

"She had kids, man."

"Fuck those kids..."

I should have punched him in the face and gotten the hell out of there, but, I knew, if he went down for this, I would go down too. "Look, Trinity said she just took off, right? Ran out of her house and didn't tell her mom, or anybody else, where she was going—and busted up her phone so they couldn't find her, right?" I couldn't believe how easily the pieces began to fit together in my mind. "So, if we can get rid of her car and dump her body somewhere it will never be found—like out at sea—it will be like she was never here. Like she just vanished off the face of the fucking earth."

A wolfish grin swept across Mark's face. He knew no one would miss her, not really. "I know a spot near an old jetty where I go crabbing. It's pretty isolated, we can dump her car out there." He filled his cup with a fresh frozen daiquiri. He was as relaxed as I had ever seen him. "As far as the body... I can't take it too far into the bay in my dingy, but, if I dump her near the channel, the tide should do the rest."

All we could do was drink, do more crystal, and wait until the sunset crowd all left. Then Mark drove Trinity's shiny silver Dodge Challenger out to the old dock. I followed in his car and tried to keep up with the big HEMI-powered muscle car.

I wondered what she'd been willing to do to get someone to buy her a car like that. I wondered what *I* would be willing to do... Although, I didn't think anyone would be offering.

After we arrived at the old pier, we parked the Challenger in some tall marsh grass near the water with her purse, cigarettes, and broken phone inside. I even tossed in a half-empty bottle of rum and what I had left of the crystal, and then we headed back. Hopefully, the cops would think she got messed up, took a dive off the jetty, and drowned. Anything but the truth.

After we got back from dumping the car, we laid Trinity out on the bed, folded her legs up at the knees, and placed her arms straight down at her sides. We strapped everything down with duct tape, and then put her body inside a large, black plastic trash bag. For two guys who had never wrapped up a body, I thought we did okay.

Mark had a small rubber dingy with a little outboard motor tied up behind his boat. He normally only used it for short trips around the marina, but it was going to have to go to sea tonight. Luckily, for me at least, there wasn't room for both of us and Trinity, so I stayed on board after we loaded her body.

I pushed them off from the back of the boat and watched as Mark silently paddled. He didn't start the engine until he was clear of the marina. As the dingy faded into the moonless darkness, I started to wonder if we might just get away with it.

I waited there in the dark for several hours until he returned. When he did, he was exhausted and soaked to the bone, but smiling.

She was gone. Sleeping with the fishes, as the Sicilians would say. That was all that mattered.

The next day, we stayed on the boat. We waited for someone to call, or come by asking for her, but no one did. It was quiet.

But by late-afternoon, there were TV reports about a missing woman—presumed drowned. The reporter spoke sympathetically about Trinity (I guess that was her real name), and the tragedy of a good life gone bad. They even showed a picture of her. But it was from high school, before the drugs and alcohol had begun taking their toll, and the smiling blonde cheerleader in the photo looked almost nothing like the used-up crystal-queen who stepped aboard our boat the day before. They never even mentioned her kids. Poor little bastards, they were probably better off being raised by their grandmother anyway.

I nervously looked around at the other boaters in their white linen shorts and deck shoes and wondered if any of them had gotten a good look at her face or would remember if they saw it again.

Not a chance, I thought. Mark's boat was like a rotting fish in a pond, everyone avoided looking at it if they could.

We didn't talk much—so we drank. By the time the sun began to dive beneath the water that evening, we finished off the rum and vodka and were starting on the tequila.

We were drunk as one-eyed pirates when we heard a series of high-pitched squeals that sounded like a chorus of madhouse laughter.

I looked out into the marina.

A dolphin was pushing a large, dark object with its snout.

Mark saw it too—so did the rest of the sunset crowd.

As it got closer, I could see a pale, purple-spotted arm with pointy, neon-pink fingernails bobbing out from a jagged hole in the side of the tightly bound black trash bag.

Up until that point, I had almost convinced myself that we had dodged a bullet, that we were in the clear.

But as the dolphin gleefully approached the boat with its macabre bounty, I could hear Trinity's ghost whispering in my ear, "Dodge *this*."

AuthOr BiO

Twitter: @Kojak_TheWriter   Instagram: @John_C_Kojak

John Kojak is a Navy veteran and graduate of The University of Texas who grew up in oily little towns around Houston. He still lives there, with a nice woman and a mean cat. His short stories have appeared in *Pulp Modern, Pulp Adventures, Switchblade, EconoClash Review, Mystery Weekly, Crimeucopia, Blue Room Book's Stories of Southern Humor and Southern Crime Anthology, Hellbound Books' Road Kill: Texas Horror by Texas Writers Vol. 5* and Vol. *7.*

Kojak's poetry collection, *Donut Shaded Sunsets,* was put out by Uncle B. Publications in 2022.

MoRe FrOm OuR AuThORs

Balloonatics

By C. R. Abby

Bill isn't a pervert. His kink is a little different, sure, but completely harmless. It's not as risky as public sex, or invasive like fisting. He doesn't like choking. And he's not coordinated enough to satisfy multiple people at the same time. If you ask someone who doesn't know Bill or about his kink, you may call him "creepy" or "deviant," an unsafe person around children.

It's not entirely their fault. People like Bill haven't been represented in media. The few interviews you can find are done with people handpicked to look like real oddballs. People who get sexual gratification from childish things. It's not about the item itself or an age, though. Bill can go to parties and not lose control.

The temptation is there, but no more than seeing a woman with a lot of exposed cleavage.

Bill isn't a bad boy.

Bill just likes balloons.

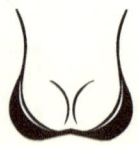

The sun is warm on Bill's face as it starts to set. He leans back into his cheap folding chair, causing the legs to sink a little deeper into the sand. The waves rhythmically wash up on the shore. Bill feels like the ocean is synchronizing with his breath. In. And out. In. And out.

This is his usual afternoon spot. It's a place where he can clear his head after a long day of work. He has a great view of the volleyball court and, just beyond that, are a myriad of restaurants and bars. Spring breakers are out now. As they drunkenly slosh around, Bill focuses on the beach ball they pass back and forth. He imagines the smell of it: plasticy and almost oily. The feel of it, slick on his fingers. The rough seam grazing his face as he puckers up to the opening where he could breathe life into it.

One of the women jumps to hit the ball over the net and slips due to intoxication. She looks up and Bill quickly turns his head, not wanting to seem like a weirdo looking at young college girls. He's not much older than them, but a slightly pouchy and graying 34-year-old. Definitely too broke to be anyone's "sugar daddy," and these girls seem expensive.

He hears the soft *ping* of the beach ball and knows the game has started again. He checks his watch and his heart flutters. He's almost late for the show. He stands unsteadily, chair still half-buried. He folds it, throws his hat and sunglasses into a tote, and slips on his flip flops before trying to speedwalk to the parking lot.

A bar down the way called Crabby's hires a balloon artist on the weekends. It's not a family friendly bar, so he has no clue whose idea it was to hire her, but he's grateful they did.

He thinks he's in love.

She is small in stature, with a voice that rings out across the bar and tickles his ears. Her laugh melts him. She was made to entertain with a bubbly aura. She is the perfect shade of hot pink. Not necessarily sunburnt, but perpetually rosy, at home in the outdoors. She ties up her frizzy blonde hair with Qualatex 260Q balloons, as those are the preferred brand among professionals for crafting little animals and hats and whatever strikes the fancy of local drunks.

She usually shows up around 7 and roams the bar area. The bar is on the beach but not as flashy as the big chains with huge tiki huts strewn with leis or totem pole faces splashed across painted wood, so tourists are few and far between. Crabby's is for the townies. Most of which are haggard fishermen or in the service industry themselves. They aren't looking for tricks or an inflatable toy to play with, they just want to get drunk and forget their day.

Its 7:25 when Bill sits at a table off to the side of the kitchen. It's much too busy for her to wander over. He's too shy to talk to her. She seems so vivacious and he's just a boring ol' cashier at a souvenir shop. He has a shitty apartment and a grumpy cat. He eats out too often. He doesn't know how to start a conversation with someone so captivating. He's enamored with her looks, sure, but he also has visions of all the dirty things they could do with the colorful party favors sticking out of her pockets. How the hell is he supposed to bring that up to her...

Bill feels something brush against his shoulder and gets a chill. He turns to see a shiny pink flower being offered to him. Then he sees a shiny name tag that says **Dana** before he looks up at her shiny lip-gloss, and finally her shiny blue eyes.

He feels his heart drop into his ass. He gapes at her, completely speechless.

"Hey," she says with a huge smile. "I see you in here all the time, but you never drink like those other guys, and I was wondering what brings a quiet guy like you into a dirty place like this? Do you want a balloon?"

His whole face heats as he tries to process what is happening. She wants to know about him? No, of course not, she's just being polite and trying to get tips.

But...she has noticed him.

Has she noticed him noticing her? The room suddenly feels very small and overcrowded. He can't breathe.

She's looking at him with spotlight eyes and he is melting under the pressure. "Sorry, I didn't mean to bother you, I just wanted to introduce myself. I'm Dana and, if you ever need a balloon artist, I'm your girl." She giggles and rolls her eyes, as if she feels ridiculous for suggesting he may need her.

But he does and he does badly.

"I'm Bill," is all he can force out.

"Oh, okay, nice to meet you, Billy." She leans in a little closer. After another moment of awkward silence, she says, "If I'm being honest, Billy, I'm just so interested in you. You always have such a contemplative look on your face...like you're struggling to hold something in, and I just want to pick your brain and know all your secrets." She laughs like bells again, self-consciously touching her polo collar. "I feel like I'm such an open book sometimes. Sometimes, I can't stop talking and I always feel like I'm going a million miles a minute and I just want to know peace like you seem to, ya know? Anyways, I think you're kinda cute."

She sits in the chair next to him. Her knees brush against his as she does so. She really is talking a mile a minute, manic and animated as she is in his lewd imagination.

He wonders if it's true, how prevalent they say coke is in the service industry, if that applies to the inflatable-manipulating fringes. Though *he* feels like the high one, starting to sweat.

"You okay? You look like you're gonna vom."

"Uh, I'm so sorry, I just spent a few hours on the beach and I think I'm a little dehydrated. Um. Yes, yes, I'd love to...chat, or whatever you'd like to do. I'm Bill." He extends a hand to shake hers and realizes he's the one rambling now. Internally, he groans. This is his chance and he's *blowing* it.

She smiles whimsically and shakes his hand. She feels so soft and warm, like a sandcastle, and he doesn't wanna let go.

"Ya know, Billy, I don't really have a set shift here. I can come and go as I please since I'm vaguely related to the owner. He's my aunt's ex-boyfriend, so, if maybe you'd be more comfortable somewhere else, we could go there and talk. I'm free all night. That sounds so exciting, don't ya think? Whaddya say?"

Bill loves hearing his new nickname roll off her tongue. *But isn't this really impulsive? She shouldn't just go with complete strangers.* He could kidnap or take advantage of her. But he would never do that, and he thinks she knows that to some degree. Although he's incredibly awkward, she is eating him up. She fills all the gaps he doesn't know how to. She is tempting the curiosity in him, scratching an itch. A need to know and touch her.

He looks up at her eyes and then back to the balloon flower she made him. *This has to be a sign, right?*

"I have an apartment not far from here."

The short car ride from Crabby's to Bill's apartment is anything but silent. Dana chatters on and on, about horoscopes and dreams and the color purple, briefly apologizing for being so bold and firmly explaining that she isn't "some kind of floozy." She's just been so bored lately and needs something to break up the monotony of her everyday life. She vibrates energy. Bill can feel it in his fingertips—perhaps that's from how hard he is gripping the steering wheel, though.

They come to a stoplight and Bill glances over at her.

Dana sighs and stretches, arms reaching as far overhead as the confined space allows.

Bill notices the hem of her shirt lifting, exposing her bellybutton. He quickly looks back at the road, trying not to think of how it reminds him of a balloon knot.

She giggles at his coy gaze. "What an absolute gentleman," Dana coos. "Are you always this polite...or is there a dark side to you?"

Bill gulps.

She laughs. "Oh, relax, Billy, I'm only teasing. Unless you want to noodle around. I'm truly up for anything."

"Anything? I doubt that," Bill responds, a bit ashamed.

"I've been known to try anything at least once."

Bill looks at her now. Really takes her in. His eyes linger on her glossy lips and he thinks about how they would feel on his. He thinks about her soft legs rubbing against his, under bedsheets. He looks at her bouncy curls again, a few long, skinny tying balloons draped over her ear like a pencil. Then he can't help but think about her bare, tan-lined tits pressed against a balloon and how gorgeous they would look. She feels like a magnet pulling him in. He unconsciously leans toward her, tightening their distance for a kiss.

"The light is green, Billy," she says with a smirk.

They finish the drive home quietly.

Bill's cat, Pim, greets them at the door, loudly purring.

"Oh, hiii, babyyy." Dana picks him up and pets him all over as Bill begins opening a can of seafood medley for him.

Not the sexiest smell, but if Pim doesn't get what Pim wants, neither will he. Pim's one to howl and headbutt for dinner, guest over or not.

"That's Pim. Found him roaming my work parking lot one day. He seemed kind of lonely. I was also kind of lonely, so it just made sense to bring him home I guess."

"I love him," Dana says, kissing Pim all over.

Bill feels a brief wave of jealousy wash over him, quickly followed by embarrassment. Looking down, Bill realizes he's still in his swim trunks. "Excuse me while I change. I'm sandy." He opens his bedroom door—and immediately slams it shut. *Oh, fuck.* He forgot.

At any given point in time, Bill has 15 or so inflated balloons he likes to bounce around and play with. Usually before bed, when the mood strikes him. Today, however, he filled *every* balloon he had, about 60. Including his two Qualatex24s, the biggest balloons he owns. They completely cover his bedroom floor. Shades of blue and yellow, pinks and oranges. Some are spotted, some are more pastel, but all are latex. He always shuts the door to keep Pim out, but also to trap the smell in.

Balloons, of course, smell like latex. Better than doctors' gloves, some nights not good enough to replace a woman's perfume and musk. But there's also an oily undertone, reminding him of bikinied girls baking in the tan. Sometimes, the smell alone can make Bill feel euphoric.

Right now, it induces panic.

"Is everything okay?"

Fuckfuckfuck. Do I say it's a prank, birthday party leftovers? But then she'll think I have live-ins, maybe a girlfriend. "Yeah, it's just such a mess in there..."

"You should see my rooms. Looks like a bomb went off in there. I don't know why I have a closet because all my clothes end up on the floor."

Bill tries to think past the distraction of her clothes on his floor. He *has* to keep her in the living room. That's it, that's fine. They can just sit on the couch and watch TV. Oh, but that's boring. What if things start to heat up? They can't "noodle around" on his sad little thrift-store couch, not with Pim watching all judgey. Cushions all flat and stained with years of God-knows-what.

He's just not ready to explain to the balloon artist that he can't help but get his cock hard when he thinks about her bouncing up and down on his colorful collection.

He's not ready, but he feels there's no way out of this. He has to rip the Band-Aid off and end his suffering.

Bill tries to drink her in before she undoubtedly leaves with the horrible knowledge of his dirty secret. He opens the door, and a medium-size yellow balloon glides out, tapping her rounded shoe.

"Oh," she says softly, "that's so funny. Seems I can never escape work, haha."

"You don't understand." Bill sighs heavily as he opens the door all the way. He's never been more exposed. More balloons fall out of the doorway. As much as he regrets it, the smell hits him and, somewhere deep down, just under the anxiety, is the itchy feeling of arousal. "You can leave. I understand. I won't go to Crabby's anymore. You'll never see me again."

Dana, still cuddling Pim, lets him down and walks into the open doorway. She assesses the space and takes it in before she finds a Q24 sitting on his bed. "Oh my God, Billy, this is perfect!" She points to the beast resting on his pillow. "Something purple, remember? From my dream! It's a sign that I was meant to come here. Why do you have all these anyway? Was there a party?"

"No," he whispers. Regret seeping from his pores. "I have...a balloon fetish. I mean, I don't want to fuck the balloon. It's more like...a tool? Like foreplay. It's complicated." He is shaking.

"Oh, well, tell me all about it. Why balloons?"

She isn't disgusted?

Bill walks into the room, feet feeling like they're a thousand pounds. He's grateful she's being polite. Perhaps he owes her an explanation. It's too late, he can't hide anymore. "When I was young, maybe ten...my family took a trip to the beach. It was May, not quite summertime but hot enough to warrant the trip... My brother and I were on the shore, digging for pirate treasure. The wind blew some confetti our way and we were so excited to have 'struck gold.' Hah. Well, I looked in the direction of the confetti and saw a wedding planner scurrying around, fussing over details that really made no sense to me. Napkins or something. Next to her, I saw a woman blowing up balloons and taping—or *trying* to tape—them to the chairs they set out."

Bill sits on the bed and Dana joins him. She takes his hand and, for the first time all night, he feels some tension relax. She may not want to fuck him anymore but at least she gives him the opportunity to get this off his chest before she calls him a freak and leaves.

"At first, I tried not to stare at her. It felt rude, you know. She had on a pink string-bikini top that seemed much too small for a wedding. But again, I was a ten-year-old boy, so I wasn't complaining. I watched her, I ogled at her, as she blew up the balloons by mouth. It was so...erotic, I guess. I watched her chest go up and down as she breathed into these balloons. Her lips puckered and she even gently moaned. Not with any purpose behind it. You know how it is sometimes, when you blow hard into something?'

Dana nods.

"Well, I watched her as she worked. I don't even know if I was fully aware of why I was watching her. I just knew it made me feel something. I couldn't look away. Until she blew one too far past its expansion point and it popped loudly in her face. She was shocked but recovered quickly, maybe a little agitated at the inconvenience. I, however, did not. I hated the sound. It disrupted my experience. It was alarming on my ears. It turned her pretty face sour for a moment. That's how I learned I'm not a popper."

"What's a popper? Calls to mind those smelling salts in gay clubs," she lightly giggles.

"Well, there are generally two groups of looners—that's what they call people like me, who like balloons. Anyway, poppers and non-poppers. Some people like the popping. It's like a building of anticipation thing. And there's all different ways to pop too, like with your teeth, or a pin, or even a lit cigarette or candle. But I'm not interested in any of that. You can't have your cake and eat it too, I guess."

"I see. I hate it when *I* accidentally pop a balloon too, but that's usually because I have to restart my sculpture. Do you like the squeaking sound? Because sometimes that annoys me."

"I like the squeak. It's all a sensory thing. I like the sound and the smell and the taste."

"Do you lick them?" Dana asks with a laugh.

"Well, no, but when you blow them up, you get a taste."

"Do you want to lick me?" she asks much more seriously.

Bill can't respond. Not by the time Dana leans into him and kisses him with so much passion, he literally can't breathe.

She is as soft as he imagined. Her mouth is gentle and slow. He feels a tension building in his sandy swim trunks but doesn't move for fear of exposing himself.

They linger there for a peaceful moment, exploring each other with curious hands. If they stayed like this forever, Bill would die happy.

"I once grinded on my teddy bear so hard that I came," Dana blurts as she pulls away from him.

"What?" Bill asks, still recovering from the kiss.

"Well, I just thought, since you shared so much, I should share something too, so it's even."

"Thank you." Bill's smile goes from awkward to authentic. "I appreciate you giving me a chance. I've never told anyone about this."

"I told you, I'll try anything once. A try-sexual." She winks. "Would you turn on some music? I have an idea."

Bill turns on the TV in the corner of his room and flips to YouTube. He finds a slow jazz mix set to ambient rain sounds. Maybe it's corny but he doesn't know what music Dana likes and this is his default. He looks at her and she shrugs her approval.

Then Dana peels off her shirt. She throws it down and it lands on a blue-speckled balloon before rolling onto the floor. She slowly unbuttons her tight jean shorts and rolls them off too, leaving her standing in a black-lace bra and sheer-pink thong.

Bill finds it cute that she doesn't match. She was as unprepared as him.

Her hips start rolling along to the deep sounds of the soulful instruments. Bill is hypnotized. He watches as she moves with the music. He can almost see the notes wrapping themselves around her, getting tangled in her energy. She gracefully bends down and plucks a red balloon from the floor.

It was fully inflated before Bill left for the beach this morning but has lost air over the course of the day.

"Have you ever had a balloon dance before? I've seen it done at strip clubs..."

"I've never been to a strip club."

"You're so sweet. Just sit there, I'll do all the work."
Dana's eyes glow with something devilish and Bill is painfully
aware of how tight his trunks are getting.

She sets the balloon on his open lap, the balloon
whispering against his obvious erection. Facing him, she lifts a
leg and rests it on the bed beside them. The translucent red
balloon is sandwiched between their hot bodies. Bill is grateful for
the pressure and, as Dana begins to grind down on the balloon, he
sees that she is too.

The balloon is pliable and fills any gap between them,
shifting as Dana does. Bill leans back onto the bed. As he does, he
looks at the balloon between them. He can actually see the outline
of her sex through the balloon, though a little obscured from the
color. He can also see his own desire pressed against the bottom
of the balloon, building a mound visible within the sex toy
between them.

He reaches out to hold her hips and gingerly guide her.
The sensation is too much. Every inch of his body is tingling. He
realizes if they don't switch positions soon, this is going to turn
into a very short dance.

Bill directs Dana onto the Qualatex24. She strips
completely, throwing her wet thong at Bill, who exhales a pained
moan. The Q24 is strong enough to support her weight so she can
ride and grind and bounce while Bill watches. He loosely strokes
himself, enough to ease the throbbing but not enough to cum.
Dana is slick with arousal and slides easily across the surface that
purples under her shadow.

There is a soft squeak where her dry skin catches the latex,
but she doesn't seem to mind. She leans to the side and grabs two
smaller balloons, a yellow and a white, and presses them against
her breasts. Bill can tell she doesn't know what to do with her
hands, but he appreciates the effort.

They continue like this for a while, trying different
combinations of balloons on different wet and dry body parts.
They press the balloons between them, sit on them, Dana even
licks a few just to be silly and Bill laughs in his ecstasy. They kiss
deeply. Hands tangle in fistfuls of hair. Skin is licked and bitten.
Dana marks Bill as hers when she scratches down his back,
leaving red hot trails where her nails were. Bill nips at her vanilla
skin and licks everywhere. They taste each other and satiate that
hunger that's been festering since they met at the bar.

Slut Vomit Vol. II

But if Bill is being honest, it's been weeks of this aching. As they reach the peak together, they moan loudly. Sweat gathers at their temples. They grasp each other desperately—until they can't hold off any longer and crash into each other like a sweeping ocean wave. Like the wind that brought confetti and the makings of a fetish to him on the beach all those years ago.

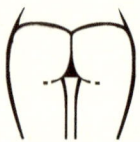

Bill wakes up in an empty bed. He isn't sure when they fell asleep and he certainly didn't feel Dana leave. As he hovers between sleep and wakefulness, he wonders if he dreamt it all. Awareness slowly seeps into his limbs. His mouth is dry. He finds enough strength to roll over and push himself up. He spreads his toes on the cold floor and rolls his head, neck cracking. Age is creeping up on him. Sadness flickers inside him. Another day with nothing to brighten his home but balloons.

She left without a word. He hopes he didn't offend her. Hopefully, her introduction to him and his balloon kink wasn't too jarring. Can he be seen at the bar ever again or has she run off and told everyone how weird he is?

Bill decides he doesn't care. There was something so liberating about telling Dana about his desire. He's buried it so deep, some days he feels like such a recluse. Like so many aspects of his life, Bill keeps himself hidden. He feels so much shame. Hollow, deflated. He's tired of it. Even if Dana is just a dream, he feels some of her vibrancy has rubbed off on him. Maybe he can be free like her. Not completely—she is absolutely, magnificently wild. But he doesn't feel like he has two heads anymore. He just needed to be seen.

Bill meanders into his kitchen for a glass of water. As he stands at the sink and looks into the living room, he chokes on his beverage. On the coffee table sits a large pink cock and balls fashioned out of twisting balloons. Squinting in confusion, he walks over, water in hand. He takes a large gulp and sees a note resting on the phallic gift.

In girly cursive, the purple ink says, **Had a great time, see you at Crabby's. XOXO, your balloonatic.**

Author Bio

Sites: Outcast-Press.com   PopCapGames.com

C.R. Abby is a returning writer from *Slut Vomit Vol. I* with her GILF (*Gin, Impatiens, & Lavender Flamingos*) story set in the notorious Florida retirement community simply dubbed The Villages. If you just want to sample the first *SV* book, such is available as an e-story on Kindle and Outcast-Press.com. In her free time, Abby weaves together modern goth blankets and uses sparkly slime as a cleaning utensil. She knows how to catch crayfish and can read the stars.

Abby is looking forward to entertaining you just as much in *Slut Vomit Vol. III*

The Doxxing Domme

By Dan Baltic

Joshua was going to pay her to doxx him. Or not exactly to doxx him, but to threaten to doxx him, to tease him about the prospect, to dangle the possibility of total career ruination and family disintegration over his head like a rainbow sword of Damocles. And unlike some of the specialists in her particular field of work—skinny little lambs subsisting on a diet of ketamine and Doritos—Leah Goldberg, the so-called Doxxing Domme, was a woman in full.

Though online commentators railed against Leah's sociopathic doxxing campaigns and cringe music videos, all topics eventually returned to the meat of the matter: Leah's "Khazar Milkers." No matter the nature of one's personal sexual aesthetics, it could not be denied that Leah, quite simply, had big fucking knockers, fat milkers swelling with the business of life, simultaneously obscene and beautiful and guaranteed to bring the men of the village to parade attention. But not all men wished to stand. Faced with the intoxicating femininity of Leah's mammal tummy and ham hock thighs, some men wished only to kneel, to sit and beg Leah to forgive them for their unwoke opinions and so-called white male privilege.

But Leah was not the type of woman to simply forgive a man his trespasses. No, Leah was far more likely to sing about his trespasses in one of her popular OnlyTok reaction videos, making strange and even demonic faces into the camera as she channeled the spirit of John Oliver and Attila the Hun. All while wearing skintight clothing such that her milk-hard nipples were visible through flimsy fabric, entrancing viewers while she sang of the crimes of white men against a weak and trembling humanity, rhapsodizing about their employers and home addresses, their wives and children, all who should have known better than to associate with a man such as their husband, father, or employee.

"I don't think we should defund the police," said Joshua, an excited tremor racing along his words. "In fact, well, you told me that I should admit something shameful? And I don't consider not wanting to defund the police shameful, but I also get really angry when I see protestors blocking traffic, especially the overweight, pink-haired lesbian types. I just can't stand them. And part of me, not all of me, not the real me, but part of me wants the car to push through and run them all over. Like that fat girl in Anaheim who wasn't even hit by the car but still had a heart attack and died. I mean, I hate to say it, but...what a fucking bitch, you know? Out there saying she's protesting fascism but, really, she just hates people who look like her father, her brother, whomever. She hates herself but, boy, does she love black people and crippled people and all sorts of sex freaks. Because those are the good people, the sex freaks."

As Joshua told her his lived experience, Leah's expression read like a Geiger counter, registering resentment and disgust, her eyes and mouth twisting and turning until her plump, healthy face had become something ghastly, a mask to be worn by Viking priestesses during particularly brutal religious ceremonies.

This disfiguring rage had the intended effect on Joshua, as he went rigid in his hand, engorged flesh forming a sort of human pilot stick. But Joshua was not the captain of this ship. In truth, he was little more than a passenger, a stowaway in the engine room of a great horny vessel.

"Shall we catalogue the many ways in which you are, quite simply, a piece of shit?" asked Leah. "That wasn't a question. *I'm* going to catalogue them. And you are going to stop stroking your little fucking dick. If you cum while I'm telling you what a dirtbag you are, I swear to God, I'm going to post this video with your name and address. You got that, you soft-dick software Nazi?"

"I'm actually an accountant," said Joshua. He knew that Leah had other clients, tons of them, but he felt momentarily stung, wondering if Leah actually hated him or was just phoning it in. Most likely, she felt some level of contempt, but not so much for Joshua as for the *idea* of him, the idea that men like him existed.

"Excuse me," said Leah. "I'm so, so sorry I got your profession wrong. You're a Nazi accountant, not a Nazi engineer? Got it. But don't worry, I'll make sure I get your job title right when I tag you in the comments. Now, keep stroking and I'm going to doxx you if you cum. Isn't this fun? We're having fun!"

This wasn't just an idle threat; Leah had doxxed men for cumming too soon before. And in case anyone was wondering, the Boogle Corporation does not take kindly to their employees appearing in "fashpig humiliation videos." With this in mind, Joshua was going as slowly as he could, using deliberate, methodical strokes that would keep him away from the erotic edge.

But Leah was intent on pushing him closer and closer, urging him to unleash his "Panzer pudding," which, in truth, was a very nice touch and invited reconsideration of her education and overall knowledge base. Joshua had assumed that Leah held little to no knowledge of military history and civilizational conflict, other than whatever nonsense her professors had imparted in classes such as "Queer Perspectives on the Second World War" and "Raceplay in Post-Colonial Cinema." But perhaps Leah was more learned than he had thought. The prospect of this happy harpy reading Gibbon was almost too much for Joshua to bear as he felt that familiar feeling bubbling up in his balls.

"Mustache-dick!" said Leah. "Are you really about to cum already?"

Leah had previously revealed that she thought Joshua's penis was small and thin like Hitler's mustache. Though Joshua didn't very much like to think about Hitler's mustache while he was masturbating, he never objected to the outrageous nickname because he feared any such complaint would chill Leah's sadistic creativity: a powerful but temperamental force for which he was paying $200 per hour. And truth be told, the thought of Hitler's mustache was acting as a helpful erotic decelerant, causing Joshua's semen to settle back down into his prostate as he contemplated the hairy rectangle wedged between the nose and lips of the notorious Austrian leader.

"Trust me," said Leah, "you really don't wanna cum until I say so." As Leah was speaking, she began to lift her tight blue crop top over her head to reveal large, milky orbs straining against an almost childishly pink bra. Though flimsy and girly, Leah's bra was doing the work of a mighty dam, holding back the rushing flow of her fertile river. "Because if my fashpig cums before I give him permission," said Leah, "his little piglets will go hungry. And you don't want the little piglets to go hungry, do you? You don't want Boogle to learn about your support for policies that would place queer folks and people of color in physical and psychological danger, do you?"

The prospect of his children learning of their father's unpalatable political opinions and then falling into poverty did not have the dampening effect on Joshua's arousal that one might have expected. Joshua had long ago made peace with the fact that man is a complicated beast, that his loins might love what his heart did hate, that anathema provided a thrill that tender kisses could not hope to replicate.

"Piglets gonna starve cause daddy likes to cum!" said Leah, as she began bouncing up and down and shaking her large breasts, the pink bra now but a fig leaf against the undulating meat. "Piglets gonna starve cause daddy loves woke pussy!" As Leah's bouncing approached a point of frenzy, she relieved her struggling pink bra of its impossible burden, unleashing her big cans. Her red nipples swung into view and Joshua's penis started shooting rope after rope of hot seed into the air, exploding in the space between Joshua and the screen.

As the semen left his body, reason entered the gap, filling his brain with concerns that had been wholly absent while he was pumping his penis for the so-called Doxxing Domme. Joshua knew that in his eagerness to have the most embarrassing, pathetic, and immoral of orgasms, he had gotten himself into a bit of a pickle. Would Leah really make good on her threat to share this video on her extremely popular OnlyTok channel, alerting the world to his regrettable perversions and fascistic opinions?

"Wow, that was really something, Leah," said Joshua as he began wiping the mess from his stomach and home office desk. "As always, you knocked it out of the park."

Joshua was about to segue into a polite but hasty goodbye when he noticed that Leah had a glassy, almost compassionate look in her eyes. It was the same expression Joshua's college girlfriend wore when she told him she needed to grow as a person. But Leah didn't need Joshua's permission to grow as a person. They had a business relationship. And Joshua knew from personal experience that it was grave, indeed, when a business partner began to show some form of tenderness.

"I'd like to just wish you a good rest of the weekend," said Leah, "but you said some really disturbing things this time. I feel like I have a responsibility to the community to consider. And a responsibility to you, to make sure you get the help you need."

Leah seemed genuine, but Joshua knew it was all layered in levels of irony and cynicism, thirst for gain masquerading as sincere attachment. But this malevolent nesting doll aspect of Leah's personality was part of what Joshua found so attractive: She was at once a hedonist and an ideologue, a globalist predator and a Hero of the Soviet Republic. And most of all, she betrayed no hint of understanding the contradictions inherent in her jollily abominable disposition. She claimed to love all, but delighted in tormenting men like Joshua. She claimed to despise toxic masculinity, but loudly fantasized about a black rapper most well-known for throwing his girlfriend off a second-floor balcony.

Why didn't Leah want to be Joshua's "white hoe"? And why did Leah's steadfast refusal to uphold any of the tenets of civilization arouse Joshua so greatly? The truth was that Joshua saw within Leah a glimmer of something not inhuman, but all *too* human, the distant moral past of the species. For instance, a lioness enters estrus when her mate and cubs are slaughtered by a rival male. And though Leah was no lioness, evolution has a long memory.

"How much will it take?" asked Joshua.

"Excuse me?" said Leah, her face morphing into a caricature of dignified offense, but her eyes betraying something a bit more calculating.

"How much to keep this video between us?" asked Joshua, sketching the contours of their developing deal.

"I told you," said Leah, straightening her posture such that her breasts rose ominously, like commercial blimps repurposed for military uses. "I have an obligation to protect the community from troubled people with the wrong ideas."

But with this proviso, the air seemed to escape from Leah's righteous façade. She relaxed her shoulders, causing her giant cans to sink into a louche hang, like cargo containers bobbing in the ocean.

"So, I can't simply accept a one-time payment in exchange for refraining from posting this video," continued Leah. "But perhaps, I could consider performing short monthly check-ins to confirm you're not a danger to yourself or others. And of course, I would have to be compensated fairly for the labor I performed in connection with these wellness check-ins."

"Fairly," said Joshua. "Of course."

Joshua and Leah regarded each other through the magical window of the Internet. In the silence, Leah idly pulled at her plump nipples, staring at the camera with the rude mammal confidence of a housecat that had just wet the carpet and dared you to react.

"$200 per check-in session?" asked Joshua.

"$1,000," replied Leah.

"Okay," said Joshua, after a moment's hesitation. "I guess I'll see you next month."

Leah's eyes had widened slightly when Joshua assented to the increase. She seemed simultaneously elated and regretful, probably wishing she had asked for more and making a mental note to do so in the future.

One-thousand dollars was a lot, but Joshua wasn't an accountant. He didn't work for Boogle, and his name wasn't Joshua. He was the CFO of a small but highly respected venture capital fund. Monday morning, he would attend a panel on the impact of systemic racism in tech hiring practices and nod approvingly as the panelists discussed how the industry needed to empower queer black programmers.

But all the while, he would be thinking about Leah's big fat knockers bouncing on the savanna, the "Doxxing Domme" greedily rutting with the strongest of the breed.

AuthOr BiO

Twitter: @Baltic_Dan

Dan Baltic is author of *NUTCRANKR,* his hilarious debut novel about men and women as chronically online as here, with the backdrop of college campuses and political protests. A sequel is in the works! Baltic is fearless leader of the Nut Army, and co-host of the New Write podcast.

Keep up to date with his brilliant and lascivious satire shorts through the Baltic State on DanBaltic.Substack.com.

More From Outcast Press

Undercover club kid Ambrose has grown up after pretending to blend in with rich college kids and falling in love with a married artist. But now new problems include finding his missing dominatrix boss, figuring our if his fiancée is more into his French female coworker than him, and dealing with the emotions that arise when visiting his incarcerated little brother his family all but forgot about.

And did we mention ties to the Russian mafia? Covering up a murder while keeping hot heads out of a double love triangle? All this and more available via Amazon, Kindle, Barnes & Nobel, Target, Outcast-Press.com, and more!

Toppings

By Brandon Mead

I've had worse coworkers. Overall, the most annoying thing about Arthur is that he always asks for anchovies on the pizza. Like he's some sort of '90s cartoon character. Like his job is fighting crime from a sewer. Like he is the only one in the room whose pleasure matters.

On the rickety bistro table that the director keeps calling "craft services," fish heads poke through solidified mozzarella. Between pillars of off-brand soda, every greasy slice Arthur hasn't consumed from the branded cardboard box is going cold. For so many reasons, I wish he would have asked them to order something with pineapple for both of us to share. But controversial toppings or not, I won't be eating any food until all of this is over.

In the middle of this terrible pizza party are two queen-sized beds and one camera. Just as obligatory as the standard hotel suite "cuck chair," JP's tripod is set up in the corner. Everyone in this room knows he won't use it.

What the man who is effectively my manager does between going handheld, is set the scene before the scene. He brings out high-wattage bulbs on C-stands, checks the white balance, uses an old-school light meter in any area he thinks

Arthur may throw me. Sometimes, to the metal barn-doors of his ARRI kit heads, he even attaches different colored gels with clothespins he likes to call "C-47s." Between his thick fingers, in the hue of dark blue with just a sliver of pink, he squeaks open wood tensioned with a silver spring. "Trade secret," he says, holding the renamed clothespin under too much pressure. "Easier to bill when it sounds legit."

I met JP in the parking lot of the university where I was about to lose my Musical Theatre scholarship. In those days, we both had bleach-blond tips, and consumer-grade digital video captured the moment he asked me the question that changed my entire life: What do you like about acting?

The first time I sucked a cock on camera, I rubbed the precum off with the sleeve of my flannel. I didn't know guys could get that wet. It all seemed much messier than I'd imagined. Saltier. Stickier.

In the retro Winnebago that JP rolled from campus to campus, the sheetless twin mattress on its floor felt like theater in the round. Hunched over until I found a more comfortable spot on my knees, by the time this guy's mushroom head bumped into the semi-permanent retainer my parents were making payments on, I was focused. Nothing mattered. Not JP whispering directions to us, not the potential audience, not even breathing.

I concentrated on my moans, my slurping sounds, getting air through my nose when I had the opportunity. The dude didn't shoot in my mouth the way JP wanted him to, but he still paid us what he promised. Hot sperm dripping down the two twenties and ten in my fist, the director asked me if I'd do it again. I told him, timecode running in the lower third of the frame, next time, I wanted to top.

There's this thing about stage fright. People talk about it like it only happens in the dressing rooms and wings. As if the second that character's shoes hit polished hardwood, it all disappears. Tension melted by red velvet, fear dissolved by tungsten rays and rolling sets. According to my teachers, the only blackout I was supposed to experience was between scenes. During standing ovations. Before accepting my Tony award.

There are no classes for tunnel vision. No workshops on vertigo. No tutorials for learning how not to turn into a fainting goat when you're between the frame of a proscenium arch.

The first time I shot in a real studio, they gave me lesbian porn to watch. Lesbian in the way that all of the girls had acrylic nails. Shaved vulvas. More silicone in their chest than realistic fat around their hips. When I asked the sound guy if I could get something with a hard dick in it, something aspirational, he laughed, "I thought you were straight."

With more half-empty Starbucks cups in the room than people who actually wanted to be there, everyone was waiting on me. This tan dude with a hairy back, who I'd only shook hands with an hour before, sprawled himself across a heart-shaped love seat. He used both hands to spread his asshole and, in character, said, "Hurry before my wife gets home."

When I woke up, JP was in my face. The furry dude was behind him, crunching Doritos between his front teeth.

"Change of plans, kid," JP said gently. "I think you may be a bottom."

That's when I got the crash course on taking dick. No eating at least 24 hours before a scene. Use a disposable enema when you don't have a shower attachment or bulb. In a pinch, a single condom and a plastic water bottle can be turned into a very effective douche. "Work with what you have. MacGyver it," JP said.

He taught me all the tricks to make the water run clear so I could be filled colon-deep with real and polyurethane cock. Never use the saline solution that comes with the kit. A little lube goes a long way. Don't just sweep the foyer, clean the whole mansion. Wipe down the baseboards, organize the cupboards. You never know how deep a house guest is going to explore.

Then the little otter with nacho cheese hands had me on all fours. Pulling my hair, slapping my face. Telling me what a sissy slut I was for craving his cock.

I didn't have to get hard or even find my camera. The work fell on the dom. If my face was blocked, he moved it to the light. If I was closing my eyes too long, he pulled them open. And after ramming my hole so wide open that I could feel cold air on my insides when the sound guy switched the A/C back on, JP smiled. "You're going to need a name."

More thought goes into a well-crafted porn alias than most people know. It's not just your first pet's name combined with the street you grew on. For men, it's typically an intentionally misspelled color or metal. Sometimes an animal. Predator or prey, depending on the role you play. If you flip fuck, it's something rough mixed with something soft. Telegraphing the ability to be versatile. Both Sock and Buskin. Subliminal drama masks printed across the case for *Pig Breeders 6* or *Nasty Boys 11*. Meticulously captioned on free sites that give viewers everything but the money shot.

Point is, whether it's a hashtag or model page, the goal is to brand yourself in two words. To make sure people clicking your scenes already know exactly what you're willing to do before they see you do it.

Like Hardy Blackwell, who almost exclusively does interracial gangbangs. Fisting legend Torque Galaxy, who has an ass like deep space and just wants your elbow grease. Or my current costar, Arthur Alloy, who gets hard as a medieval sword and shows no mercy.

His knighting was sometime after he asked to be called T45 which, apparently, is one of the strongest grades of steel. Back before I was in the industry, when he told JP, "It's how they built the space shuttle, man!"

According to the small crew the director has left, JP told Arthur, reliable mechanical properties or not, to settle on something that didn't make him sound like a sympathetic robot with an Austrian accent.

Today, in the muscular shadow of The King of the Round Craft Services Table, JP says, "You ready to shoot or what?"

My Lord the Twinkinator nods, he's programmed and prepared to destroy.

To me, while I eye half a bag of stale barbecue chips and room-temperature lemon-lime Gatorade like a reward, JP says, "Feenix, good to go?" Because in this hotel room that's who I am, Feenix Blu. The totally legitimate name of a man who is ready to take a beating that leaves his body bruised in every shade of cerulean, then rise from the ashes.

The production starts like most of them. Talent sitting thigh to thigh against the headboard of whichever bed isn't being used to stage the empty lighting cases and camera bags.

JP asks how we identify and we give scripted nervous laughter until we say in unison, "Straight."

The director wants to know how many times we've done this before and, after Arthur answers, I make sure my teeth are showing when I say, "One-hundred and sixty-seven."

Behind the camera, JP rolls his eyes. My disappointed father figure who knows I just make up numbers. The middle-aged pimp who paid for my retainer to be removed and just wants to see me succeed. A boss fighting to keep us relevant in a world where the lines of sexuality continue to blur.

At least, as much as the industry has changed, men's desire to lust after what seems unattainable has stayed the same. The way heterosexual men like lesbian porn, what homosexual men enjoy about the fantasy of fucking a straight guy is the challenge. Gamifying sex. Being gay on Hard Mode.

What these men like about me isn't just that fantasy though. It's the idea that a straight guy could like fucking men so much, he just can't stop doing it. That he'd keep pushing his limits, let it get rougher and rougher.

Interview over, me and Arthur Alloy are committing ourselves to historic gay BDSM cinema. Taking roles that should be going to men who do this for free three nights a week in the privacy of their own home.

We're not kissing as much as swapping salvia. He's spitting in my open mouth so he can suck it off my tongue and project it back onto my face. I don't mind. The thing about working with The Twinkinator is, he doesn't waste time. And the sooner I get his load, the sooner I can eat something.

"On the ground," the King demands. He tells me to keep my hands behind my back. To throat his sword to the hilt. If I fail to do either, the wide part of his giant palm lands hard on my cheek, long fingers cupping over my ear like an explosion.

The blocking is a blur. I'm back on the bed, pressed to the dirty hotel carpet, slammed against the wall. My pay is the highest in the room but my only job is to do what I'm told.

While JP follows along, I feel heat in my ribs, my throat, my ass. Arthur, whose real name I've never asked about, plugs my nose with his index finger and thumb while he shoves his entire length down my windpipe and pumps. "You don't need to breathe," he says. "You need to suck this cock."

I try to relax, to not choke against my stud's pubic hair when he moves a single finger to the tip of my nose and pushes up until my nostrils flare. "Good piggy-boy." I don't want to see pieces of the cheese sandwich I ate yesterday again when he curves his thumbs into the side of my mouth like hooks and pulls me back and forth on his cock. I'm projecting positive energy that my vocal warmups counteracted the sip of water I had for breakfast when my coworker kicks a black boot into my balls and reminds me, "Eyes up here, boy."

The artist formerly known as T45 looks down at me. Stringy spit falls with intention from his mouth to my forehead when he says, "Tell me you're a good faggot."

In response, my stomach growls. I'm trying to stay in the moment but all I can think about is how hungry I am. How I wish that swallowing cock really meant swallowing. That in a totally non-cannibalistic way the meat of Arthur's impressive shaft could make a decent meal.

Then I remember how many times he already had his dick in my ass.

Cleaned out with the full bag of tricks or not, I'll be thinking of him in a few days if my intestines start to hurt more than usual. If I go back to the doctor to learn I have E. coli in my guts and have to wonder if it was the ass-to-mouth or just the single leaf of romaine lettuce from my final meal. The last thing I want to do is explain to some cute nurse that I'm risking what presents as extreme food poisoning just because I want a jet ski.

"Say it," the King commands once more.

I shake myself back into reality. With my mouth and throat full, I murmur the five syllables. Tears stream from the corner of my eyes. I can't remember the last time I had a full breath. Just like being on stage, my workplace fills with black. All I can see is JP over Arthur's shoulder doing a POV shot. He's winking at me. Telling me, *You've got this, kid.*

In the center of the vignette, I remember what JP said he saw in me. The ability to look like I am both devastated and excited. Intrigued but frightened. Bewitched by my own sexuality while simultaneously looking like I'd rather be anywhere else in the world. According to JP, the best porn stars are the ones who make planned submission look like exploitation. "That innocent sparkle in your eye is something that cannot be taught," he'd say. "You were made for this."

In the trance of submission, an hour could pass. Two hours. All I know is that my ass feels wide open and I'm dripping from an unidentifiable combination of liquids.

Bending down, Arthur pulls at my nipples hard. "Do you think you've earned this load?"

While I wince in pain, I watch his cock and balls swing heavy between his boots. Instruments of reproduction repurposed for demolition. I use my begging voice when I say, "Please. Please, Sir."

He's back in my mouth, thrusting hard and pulling out to stroke himself, using my tongue for lube whenever he wants. Any extra saliva coming from my mouth, he grabs to rub on my face and laughs, "Such a messy boy. Are you hungry?"

Starving. Ready to eat anything. If he is going to cum down my throat, so be it. I don't know if a throatpie counts as dessert. More likely cum could be classified as soup or a warm beverage, but I'd take it. "Feed me, Daddy," I get out between being face-fucked.

"It's coming boy," he says, body tensing. He tugs at his balls.

I position myself, knowing I'm seconds away from curbing my hunger pangs. Sustenance will be mine.

Without a free hand to force them wide, my co-star reminds me again, "Open your eyes." It's smart because we don't want to have to take it again. Put cold cream of mushroom soup or coconut milk in a syringe to fire into my mouth on a reshoot. It would be edible, but it could also take the rest of the day. With a few more strokes, Arthur adds, "Hold them open."

I obey before I think, *Clockwork Orange*ing my fingers in place. I feel the tip of his cock on my eyeball then, with a series of jolts and loud moans, I'm blind behind a curtain of white.

Before the final bow, my co-star grabs my hands and orchestrates a high-five. The video is off but we still need stills to document my desecration. He says, "Took it like a champ, bro!"

JP says, "Surprise."

The cum stings my pupils in a way that ensures I'll be going to the doctor for the steroids that treat conjunctivitis. It's salty like sea water and Arthur's favorite pizza topping. I really wish he would have ordered pineapple.

Deprived of what I anticipated being fed, my stomach creaks. Every time someone in the room says "fish eye," I think about the cold pie sitting on the table. Once they get me a wet rag, I'm eating every bite.

When JP asked me what I liked about acting, I didn't have an answer. I liked the way it made me feel, knowing people enjoyed my work. I liked being able to do something that not everyone could do. Now, I like that, with every shoot, I improve my craft. I like that today may be some of the best work I've ever done.

And with a belly full of anchovy pizza and warm drinks, maybe it's true that I'll never win a Tony. My stage is rented rooms. My props: bodies and fluids. But find me immortalized in looping GIFs of cumshots and soundbites of flesh hitting flesh. Congratulate me when I win my award for Best Sub Slut of the Year because I'll be there, smiling.

AuthOr BiO

Instagram: @FierceStoryTelling

Brandon Mead is a Best of the Net-nominated bathtub writer and intermittent poet, living on the other side of the "split life line" on his left palm. While most kids were reading about wizards, he was devouring Chuck Palahniuk and sneaking paperbacks of *My Secret Life* into summer camp.

"Transgressive fiction with a little glitter on it."

Fierce Storytelling

the writing of **Brandon Mead**

@FierceStorytelling
FierceStorytelling.com

As a former Florida man, both his fiction and nonfiction smell like the kind of orange trees that are cut down because of citrus canker. From the gloom, where he now calls Seattle home, he is working on a collection of short stories; the backbone of which is about a gay man making friends with his tapeworm. Find out more about that at FierceStorytelling.com

More From Outcast Press

Citrus Springs isn't just a bunny-dotted, zinnia-speckled city nestled in Florida's rare dewy hills. It's a state of mind, albeit an altered one. With "In Bloom" on blare, Paige Johnson gives life to the Wonderland tarts and bitter Xanax fiends who reside in tangerine dreams.

Whether these 40+ illustrated poems tell the tale of South Beach sugar babies or Bay Area scrapers-by, the characters are always in search of ecstasy, novelty, meaning. An infatuation so intense, it's psychedelic.

Girl Dinner

By Paige Johnson

I've been upgraded from bottle girl to sushi model. A human platter, buffet babe, or wanton wonton-woman, as my manager keeps whistle-singing in the kitchen. At least for the chefs' week of slash-price samplings or costly novelties known as Miami Spice. Talk about tips. More than I usually get during the SoBe Wine & Food Festival with all the other breastaurants raking in the summer tourism. In fall, I'm the belle of body shots as competition flies out or flabs up for the holidays.

I cherish the anticipation in my tummy as I strut out to a customer, the full house's attention on me as I nail the brisk burlesque in approaching the head of the table: I provide him a profile view as my stiletto slides up a table leg, making a shapely triangle of my bent knee and straight right. Then I turn at attention like a sexy soldier, let the ebony silk robe fall from my snow-white shoulders for the chefs to catch. I twirl for the appetizing jiggle, and slink back onto the table's sparkly mesh and seaweed wraps.

My expression is meant to remain neutral like a still life, but my smile is indelible.

The suited diner, likewise. "What an entrance. What a birthday present," he laughs to himself as a waiter places a small sparkler inside my belly button.

"Oh?" I perk up though I'm lying down. "*Ota ome*. Happy birthday!" I glance side-to-side but see all the chairs have been pulled.

"Party of one," he confirms as the silly candle fizzles out. "Invitations must've gotten lost in the mail."

"*Sumimasen*," I apologize.

"*Domo. Boku wa hikikomori desu. Uzai. Dasai.*"

I give the blank stare I should've from the start. "Sorry, I'm only Japanese inside this establishment." With a wink, I elaborate, "I may look like I blend in here, but I've been raised more German-American since my adoption. In fact, and quite fittingly, my classmates growing up would mispronounce my name Yummy instead of Yumi—on purpose or not."

"Ah, so you've got the other side of the Axis down, too. Your secret's safe with me. You know, my friends always say I've got the spy squint of that era—though I'd prefer to have your batch of bullying, the kind where you're accidentally—and accurately, might I add—called delicious."

I take note of his handsome but lopsided features. Perpetual suspicion on his face, one brow low and the other high, like a P.I. who has much to mull over. There's an endearing distinction to him, an attractiveness that makes me wonder more than I should entertain. About hidden features, quips, and cash.

"Don't worry," he says of my reservedness. "I ran out of foreign words too. Gave up learning after the Duolingo bird squawked at me sideways one day."

I give a small smile and admit, "Sorry if *I'm* short on chatter. Boss usually keeps us quiet, on account of being human furniture and all." I peek at the sous chef carrying a boat of soy sauce and a face full of straight lines that say he couldn't give a ~~shit~~ sashimi about whether I follow the mute rule or not. "But if you're all alone and it's what you request... I'm sure we could work something out."

"Oh. Certainly. I thought it was half the experience." He looks around as if to inform the appropriate authorities—whomever they might be—but the sticklers seem to be on smoke break.

I'm pleased to be saved of boredom by talking and potentially landing a portly tip, given the implication of his tone. I smile placidly as red-orange waterlilies find their way onto my clear pasties.

"They match your makeup," my customer comments.

"As though you came here to ogle my *eyes*." I flutter my lashes to highlight the vermillion cat-liner.

"Well, now you're making it so I have to." He smirks.

"Don't be asking for any refunds now," I tease. "If you don't eat into my 'aesthetics' to see what you want, it's your fault."

"That's a funny way to pronounce areoles."

This cracks a laugh out of me. "*You're* in a funny way."

He tips his head. "Should be. That's what they pay me the buku bucks for." He looks around. "Wait, that's not a racist saying, is it?"

"No!" I laugh so much, the chef xylophone-taps me with his chopsticks for disturbing the rainbow roll he's trying to rest over my ribs. "I think it's French. Like, *merci beaucoup*."

"Hm. Miami really is a melting pot. You know scraps of all the languages. Schools down here mustn't be just stomach pumping stations like *Girls Gone Wild* led me to believe."

I hum with thought, fake offense. "Not so fast. My ethics professor *does* steal vid lectures from Harvard instead of making an actual online class, so, we've still got that ironic Florida flavor."

He takes a sip of Suntory Toki whiskey. "Hm. Well, I like a lot of the flavors that the East and its coast have to offer."

"They can be unique or efficient," I agree, lowering my tone as a palm frond of edamame slides into the dip of my collar bones. The master chef and his apprentice position it just so.

"I see why you're often sworn to silence like a British Royal Guard," the diner commiserates, unrolling gold-tip chopsticks from embroidered linen. He looks mochi-sweet in the candlelight. His light brunet hair high-and-tight like a military man between tours. Irish features like G.I. Joe sans steroids. Pale, holdable hands like a piano player. "Thanks for entertaining me."

My jaw barely moves, throat scarcely reverberates as I talk at an even pace. That's part of the art. "It's my job. A mutual feeling... A process. Nyotaimori is body art. They say eating off a beautiful woman is a connection to all the senses, art in all its forms. It's a gift in many facets. After all, dinner's on me, a titillating table." I always give this spiel but this time it feels less like a script. More intimate than something the manager told me to use to enchant potential reviewers.

He leans further in to hear me. Or admire the tiny Siamese tulips someone sprinkles around my midsection. "Beautiful, beautiful," he says, and I feel a tingle beneath the triangle of cling wrap stealthily placed over my V.

I wonder if the translucent strip ever fogs or appears mist-tickled, if a coworker can tell, and the thought makes me blush. I change the gears of my mind: "Funny thing, since I can't usually do more than lie motionless for hours at a time...I used to keep an earbud in. Listen to an audiobook or meditation radio."

"Until?"

"Until the little black bud fell into a guest's ponzu sauce. They thought it was a bug. They got the whole meal for free, and I almost got fired."

"I'm sorry that happened to you. What trouble trying to find peace can bring."

"No need to be... I find amusement in bad luck—even while it's happening. Everything works out in the end. The way it's supposed to."

"Hmmm. I can see where you're coming from. I guess I can take some light from the darkness, too."

"Are you in the medical field?" I venture. "To say that and have the 'bookoo bucks' to eat here alone, I mean." And to have a face so soft but sort of solemn.

"Oh, no, no. No practical skills here," he ha-has. "I'm, eh, a comedian," he whispers like it's a dirty word, could cause a stir. "I really hate telling people that. They expect so much out of you then: to always be 'on' and cheery. But, well, if you can't confess things to the naked girl you're eating off, who can you trust to be nonjudgemental?"

"Well, you seem a natural to me. Open or funny... Not that you have to put on any act. You can relax. You're right, I'm not one to criticize."

In time, a busboy slides banana leaves of oshinko and snow crab cutlets over my shins. Tempura maki makes its way onto my thighs. An icy sea urchin fans over my pubic mound like spikes of hair. Though a thin layer of plastic and plant matter separates me from it, the unbalanced weight and thought of

Slut Vomit Vol. II

prodding prickles against my most sensitive area, leaves me hot and bothered yet chill-bumped.

"Appreciate it. Others might find a mealtime Mona Lisa a bit unsettling, but me, I thrive off an audience." He smirks, pinching a piece of gingered unagi between his chopsticks.

I keep my eyes stickered to him. Customer is always right. Birthday boys are surprisingly generous. "Hmmm. You have the opposite of my job. I'm all silence and stillness too often."

"What's that saying? It's better for people to assume that you're stupid than to open your mouth and prove they're right." He takes a careful mouthful, more mannered than most I've seen. "Not that I'm implying y—"

"*Ahhh.* So you tripped yourself up with your own proverb. Double paradox." I titter and watch him wipe his mouth with a glossy napkin.

He nods as he chews, presumably mulling over flavor profiles and phrases. "See. I do that quite often. So, that makes your job best."

I imagine him splayed nude on a long mahogany table fanned by spools of glass noodles and spidery kiku flowers. When my mind's eye drifts lower down his torso, past plates of sweet chili hiding a happy trail, I smile. "Best." I nod. "But maybe not worlds different when I think about it. Odd hours. Unconventional income. Interesting stories."

"Hmm. Going back to what you said about the quietness or comedown after a performance... There's a lot of hotel downtime. A lot of thin walls and mind-numbing white noise... muffled chatter and hallway clatter. I once heard a comic say, Loneliness is the gig between others."

"So, you don't get out and explore each new city? Bring a companion along?" My eyes rove down his hand for sign of a ring, or maybe just a tell-tale tan-line on the fourth finger.

He shrugs. "This is my extent. Looking for nice grub, a pretty girl to chat up. Life can be simple that way. What about you? How do you spend your time?"

I give a demure shrug. "Work. Work. Work. But it'll pay off. They'd never catch me for insider trading with all the biz deals I eavesdrop on." I wink. "This is my entertainment too. I learn bits of languages, street jokes, tales from pro skateboarders and singers and fighters. Once I even overheard a breakup."

"You gather little slices of life from all around."

"Exactly. Like you must... You're my first seasoned comic though. Tell me, are you as scared of being 'cancelled' as all the other minor celebs I've come across?"

He concedes that his humor can be crude, "push boundaries" if anyone ever wanted to cause a controversy. "But who doesn't love attention? Even in perverse ways."

We have that in common... "But even when it comes to an uppity crowd member? Here, dissatisfied customers can get handsy, but at least I have a more obvious staff for support."

He shrugs. "It's not my intention to upset anybody but I don't believe you can go too far. I mean, some people would say being a naked sushi model is going against moral decency, but that's because they don't understand the art. Besides, if someone thinks they should come into either of our work places to be offended, they're the ones who came in with the wrong idea... We try to make people look at life differently, to smile. That can't ever be wrong."

I nod slowly and let him take in the yellowtail nigiri. "That's true. We're not responsible for others' hang-ups or self-repression. Not trying to do any wrong..." Unafraid of the irony, I still wonder if he's got a girl around, any lingering chuckle-fuckers. "If you come across confident enough, I guess the pearl-clutching crowd will dissipate."

"Confidence comes in different shades. You can just fake it until it becomes a second skin."

This makes me contemplate my boldness. My hips sway slightly as I bite the edge of my lip and ask, "Plus, after a set, you'll be surrounded by a horde of admirers." The discomfort can drift away like steam. "I'm sure you've charmed the pants off a couple, right?"

His gaze flickers to my jasmine-garnished groin as if to suggest sometimes it's simpler than that. "I'm sure you have an easier time with that than me."

Smirking, I admit, "Maybe, but I've never taken that to its end. The literal sense."

He doesn't seem to react like he's imagining it, me bumping "ends" with another lounge guest. He doesn't seem to react much at all, bulldozing over my implication, plainly saying, "Ah, well, I wouldn't know either. Been married most of my career."

My teeth meet as I contemplate if this means currently. But then why wouldn't a wife be having dinner with him, at least phone in to sing 'Happy Birthday' over FaceTime like I've seen so many long-distance couples ridiculously or reluctantly do? "You know, some people would say their biggest heckler is their spouse," I say with mock lightness.

He nods over his covered mouth, a vulnerable look shadowing his face as he tries not to choke over the rosy roe pods. "Ah, yes. I can see it. Can't say I've combatted that cliché well. Or done much to evade deserving it... Ex-wife once interrupted a show to yell at me. Something about laundry and a hair tie she insisted wasn't hers. How she can tell one black circle is different from the next is beyond me."

"You must have been mortified."

He shakes his head. "No, no. I tried to turn it around and have the crowd think it was planned, a bit of a back-and-forth roast."

"And did they buy it?"

"Enough of them, maybe a majority. Doesn't matter. Entertained either way. Got paid the same amount."

I hum in thought. "That's a bit of a whore's motto," I eventually tease.

He lightens a tad.

I say, "I see why she's an ex."

He laughs at this, smirking, saying no I don't.

Quirking a brow, I expect to him to launch into more tales that prove the razzing was a mild spat.

But it's worse.

"Ahh, now there's a dark one," he says with a contemplative look in his eyes, large fingers rolling the chopsticks over his thumb. "We had something a little more permeant than a breakup... A divorce...from life... So, actually, I look back on her heckling me fondly, as a funny moment. One of the last." His smirk confuses me, proud of the misdirection.

Then I remember a phrase: Comedy is coping.

My cheeks burn like wasabi. My shoulders bristle. I stop the arm undulation before I spill something. "Oh my gosh, I'm so sorry. I didn't mean... That's so tragic," I say even though I feel myself morbidly drawn to prying out more details. Softening my voice, I ask, "Long ago?" and look around for a waiter to offer him a cup of shochu on the house, offer me a respite from the embarrassment.

"Mhm, almost a year... Touring keeps my mind off it."

Skeptically, I purse my blossom-colored lips. I bet grief comes in waves, especially alone on the road. Though I suppose there's not much choice. Medical bills still skim in through mail slats. Stress piles up and proliferates. Munchie girls still splay themselves on tables, offering to satiate just a small hunger.

Just have to keep on keeping on like a shitty song, a sonic Band-Aid, a pitiable platitude.

Clearing my throat as the second drink arrives, I quietly cheer him on with a consoling, "Kanpai."

He tilts the crystal glass towards my mouth, asking if I want a sip.

I say, "I can't drink on the job."

"Oh? What if I invite you up for a nightcap," he says, eyes drifting towards the ceiling. The Catalina Hotel is upstairs. Like plenty of guests, he has a room there. "If it makes you more comfortable, I'll drape the mini bar over you. To feel more at home—or work."

We both laugh a bit hollowly.

Though my curiosity still isn't sated and I tell myself it's for safety reasons. Maybe he retaliated on her stunt and strangled her. Maybe he was a perfectly reasonable husband but now he's widow-bitter to new girls in the bedroom. Maybe I wouldn't mind if only I had a modicum of knowing beforehand. "Oh, but your wife—"

"She wouldn't mind. She can't," he laughs like a cough, rubbing his sticks over a strip of pink sashimi.

Maybe I'm the pervert for finding it suggestive. For imagining me taken on a huge porcelain plate, my cheeks pressed into the cold surface, fingertips flexing at my sides and slipping in the decorative sauce swirls with each thrust.

I'm aware a sliver of me is turned on by the sympathy, the sadness, the danger. The slim possibility that he is responsible or unusually guilty over her death.

"You have my deepest condolences," I insist though my tongue feels fuzzy or static when I say it. Like when you take a sip of seltzer when you were expecting plain water. "I can't lie, I'm more impressed by your perseverance now. To go back on stage night after night, especially after losing a spouse... That's courageous. May I ask how she...how it happened?"

"Well, apparently...laughter wasn't the best medicine..."

I swallow.

"Also because it was a car wreck and not cancer." He still laughs darkly at the double misdirection.

My smirk is automatic if self-serving. "Oh, you're impossible!" I laugh softly, "Okay, I see why you're a comedian... You've got a gift for turning pain into punchlines. But seriously, I admire those who find humor in darkness. Most people crumble under that kind of weight."

"Your compliments... They're putting quite the sugary spin on things... It's just always been ingrained in my personality so it's not like I'm so different after the grief..."

Grief changes people, but it also brings out hidden aspects of their personality. Yet even when he goes on to tell me it was a common highway crash, I am only half-hearing. Find myself inexplicably asking if he was in the SUV when it happened.

His eyes widen a bit, rounding deliciously. "No..." he says like he isn't sure why I would ask when his body language doesn't betray something *that* traumatic. "God, thankfully I was not there... I'm surprised no one has asked me that before, but now I see it's another thing to be grateful for."

My nod dusts my flower clips against the table. "Well, that's a blessing in disguise, isn't it? I mean, no one wants to witness their partner's final moments like that." I pause, then dare to ask, "Do you think she at least went out laughing?" Does anybody? I'm not exactly sure what I'm fishing for but I like all the contours and twitches of his face when I ask these things. It feels like I'm making him as denude as me, accenting him with new little emotions like spices. It stirs a fluttering beneath and south of my navel. A tingle in my chest that tells me we're getting somewhere.

His brows raise. "I wouldn't know... Like I said, I wasn't there... Now, that you mention it, I hope so. I hope she was laughing along to a comedy station. It was like her to have SiriusXM on so maybe she was listening to *The Bonfire* or something, died happy..."

"Oh, I suspect you're right. Life is so unexpected, jarring." Tilting my head, I say, "No wonder you have such dark material. Is it off-the-cuff or written down though?"

"Half and half," he says slowly, gripping his empty glass like he's not interested in talking shop or much of anything anymore. Like I anticipated. "Things usually start written but evolve in the moment or depending on crowd reaction... It's not that I seek out dark stuff... It's that things can just be dark."

Like this conversation on a day to celebrate life.

I nod. "That's why we need to make the light in-between." I veer off my go-to lines, too. And that's where excitement thrives. But playing to a crowd of one, their orchestra box of emotions, that's always the easiest fun. The encore is always the same. The tip just inflates like a therapist's bill or the smoke bubble on a sakura martini.

When the tab is hundreds of dollars and most customers don't realize the fine print gratuity, I come out on top. Now, I'm about to come from a customer giving me top.

He moves ravenously. Tongue exhilaratingly cold from everything consumed before.

With the chill of his hotel room's cranking A/C, I feel a bit like one of the crustaceans on a bed of ice downstairs: splayed with gauzy eyes, deliciously pink from head-tip to polished toe. Even with the surgical cleaning I give myself every evening, the smell of the ocean never completely leaves my nostrils. Perhaps that's why I always act like I'm on vacation: spontaneous in spurts amid the calculating.

An edible canvas, I melt in his mouth. We melt into each other like anmitsu: sweet and tangy and textured.

If the roe pearls from dinner were an aphrodisiac, I'm an amphetamine, prompting his energy with crystal intentions. *More, more,* my open mouth demands without any words. *Again,* my hungry hands whisper. If my eagerness scares him off of cumming, it's only too quick.

Want is etched into the quick-twitch spasms, the hip-jerking and delirious repetition of our curling fingers and tongues and toes. At one point, with my eyes clasped tight to squeeze more feeling out of my skin, I imagine his lick from an ariel view, his vigor like digging the meat out of an opalescent clamshell.

This disgusts even me, yet just as soon, that shivering revulsion gifts another double-edged thrill: tingles and roils and requests for a stronger scooping.

We're sifting for that deep-seeded pearl, a release to deep-seated pining. Suck, suck, sucking up the juice, salt only heightening the crests during a dehydrated search. Voracity dribbles at the side of his smooth mouth, shiny like sea glass.

Slurping, submerging, finger-prying and -painting, wiping pearly water into the silk napkin of my inner thigh, teasing and re-tasting. Getting me to pant, pulse and see patches of starlight not filtering in from between the curtain seams.

Ah-ah-ah, I arch my back into a bow shape.

He laps all the way up to my hip bones, mapping their C-shape. Corkscrewing his digits into the sea of slime. A squelching, sloshing cave-dive. Biting the shell of my ear until I'm streaming, screaming as my mind throbs and steams, evaporating, an eye and leg twitching.

When I get him to do the same, there's a swirl of foam-green bills awaiting me on the pillow, tied and tethered in mesh-web ribbon.

But I wait until he's tuckered as though sun-sucked, limping into the bathroom, to scour for better like a greedy 'gull.

I slip the wallet from his designer jeans half-folded under the tufted white bedframe. I don't expect there to be leftover cash—what I want is less replenishable.

Replacing his wife's pocket picture with my calling card, a business card that would put Patrick Bateman to shame. I consider this souvenir swapping, a fair trade. No, an elevated one. An upgrade to less complicated exchanges. Embossed and boldface are the words **unconventional entertainer**, anyway.

I personalize the memento with a glossy fingertip dip into myself and then the **i** in **Yumi**. It's a subconscious pheromonal reminder in lieu of a sparkling gel-pen heart. A literal smear of personality, dew to dot a love letter or future sugar baby contract.

The voodoo-beauty guru girls on TikTok call it vabbing, or vaginal dabbing, an oceanic aphrodisiac perfume, but I call it an investment, artful angling. Fishing with a wider net. Casting for a catch that will always come back.

Author Bio

Facebook, Twitter & Instagram: @OutcastPress1

Paige Johnson is editor-in-chief at Outcast Press (including this very anthology). Her quirky cam girls appear in Urban Pigs Press' *HUNGER*, Cowboy Jamboree's *MOTEL*, Anxiety Press' *Mirrors Reflecting Shadows* amid others.

Johnson's debut chapbook about pills, people, and pining is called ***Percocet Summer: Poetry for Distancing Dates & Doses***. It is a four-part seasonal series, the second installment being *Citrus Springs*, about Florida, psychedelia, and other premonitions. As she strings together her third novel *Cherry, Coke & Cam Shows*, she often uploads cute quote videos on TikTok @OutcastPress.

Dead Fish

By Annabel Costello

Bunny should have known these suburbanite kinksters wouldn't want to go down to the porno theater to watch *Nekromantik* with him. From the moment they let him in on their supposed fetish, he'd known they weren't even close to being the real deal about it. That's not to say Bunny was either. No, Bunny isn't into corpse-fucking, Bunny isn't really into much of anything at all—well, except for *watching*—but it still feels like something of a letdown.

Mouths dropped in abject disgust, like Bunny was the freak. Maybe he was, to them, anyway. Meeting them the way he did. They came looking for a two-for-one deal, a stud to fuck her in all the ways she was too embarrassed to ask him to do, and a slut to let him do all the "freaky shit" she'd never let him do to *her*. Bunny could do all of that and more, guaranteed.

Leaning against the grimy-slimy wall of the theater, Bunny lights a cigarette from a crumpled packet, that he crumples even more to fit back into the pocket of his lowcut jeans, cut low enough to show off his happy trail, startlingly dark compared to the bottle-blond hair on his head. The cigarette glows cherry-red, matching the flickering neon that blinks above Bunny's head: **ADULTS ONLY.**

One day soon, the porno theater will close down and, with tears in his eyes, Bunny will probably wander up the boulevard and into a bar with a sticky floor and no lock on the bathroom door and cry into a Long Island, then get picked up by a guy who thinks he looks pretty with puffy eyes and snot running over his cola-flavored lips. Maybe he'd ask Bunny why he was crying, wipe the tears from his speckled peach cheeks and buy him another drink, or maybe he'd take Bunny home and give him something to really cry about.

Or maybe the closure would just be that last push Bunny needs to splash out on a certain home cinema setup he's been eyeing from the ads in *American Cinematographer*, the one with the surround sound speakers and a white canvas screen for the projector he'd have to build a shelf for behind his cracked white-pleather couch. He's even seen people refit their ceilings with pinprick lights to look like stars. He could do that, too, let himself fall asleep watching *Pink Narcissus*, beneath his very own sky of LED constellations.

A nondescript black Audi pulls up beside Bunny while he smokes. The window rolls down with an electric hum and a plain, L.A.-handsome face stares at him from the driver's seat.

Bunny doesn't step out to hustle, but people swarm on him like flies to honey, because they know he's drenched in it. Drenched boys like Bunny are hard to ignore. Bunny just can't turn people away from what they want, what they need, especially if they want to pay him for his honey, especially when he'd only be letting them take it for free anyway.

From the passenger seat, a plain, L.A.-pretty face leans over to stare at him, too.

Introductions are made, the two of them tell Bunny their real names, but he thinks of them as "John" and "Jane" anyway, because it's easier that way, and Bunny preens for them, flashes them his perfect porn-star smile, pretends like he doesn't know what they're building up to. John tells him, in a roundabout sort of way, that they had met a friend of a friend of a friend—"*Jimmy Fontaine, he said you guys go way back,*" John says, and Bunny thinks about a cocktail bar that he was too young to be working at and the bitter, barely-there taste of an acid tab that said **EAT ME** on his tongue—who had told them all about how cool Bunny is, about how Bunny can always be found if you know where to look, about how Bunny is always up for a good time.

Sent to him with the promise of a freebie, Bunny can tell.

"*You know, we were just on our way to a dinner reservation, would you like to join us?*" Jane asks.

Intermission is over in three minutes, and Bunny had been excited for the next flick—skin on skin, open mouths, hard and soft and wet all over—but the couple in the car are looking at him with the sort of reverence people only have for the things that fascinate yet elude them.

There was a stack of *Playboys* and *Honchos* that Bunny kept under his mattress back home, and he'd take them out to flick through the glossy pages, looking at the beautiful people with their cocks out and tits bared. He'd stare at them, turning the centerfold this way and that, fascinated at what they were doing, how they did it, fascinated that people like that really existed.

These people stare at him, from the safety of their car, fascinated that people like Bunny really exist. That pretty boys like Bunny—with bottle-blond hair and lowcut jeans that show off how they don't have tan lines and cropped shirts that show off their pierced bellybuttons and who hang around porno theaters *just asking for it*—really exist.

He waves goodbye to the mustachioed Tony in the ticket booth, who is smoking a cigarette that he holds between teeth he won't get fixed. Tony likes Bunny—"*You're a strange one, Bunny. You gotta be more careful out there*"—and had a pocketbook full of plate numbers he kept inside his motorcycle jacket. That leather jacket, boy, it made Tony smell like a *man*.

Tony nods back, pulling his book out, licking the nib of his blue biro pen.

Bunny can tell that John and Jane get a bit of a thrill being seen with him. It's in the look they give each other as he takes one last drag of his smoke, tossing it like a shooting star directly into the storm drain at the curb, before he folds himself into their back seat, bringing with him the scent of cheap cologne and the sweat of a still-hot L.A. night. Leaning back against the leather, Bunny places a hand over his toned stomach, the tip of his pinkie slipping below his waistband. *"I'm starved,"* he says.

The three of them go to a restaurant that Bunny's been to once or twice, with tricks who wanted it to feel like they were dating instead of paying him: faux-bohemian with exposed brick and French tablecloths and turn-of-the-century lightbulbs. Bunny orders calamari from the small plates menu and the most expensive cocktail they serve. "Keep 'em coming," he tells the waiter, chasing each drink with a strong shot of the bartender's choice. John and Jane order full but light meals, they smile at Bunny's antics while they sip dry white wine. Bunny passes the cheque, that gets placed squarely in the middle of the three of them, with a wink.

And then they take Bunny home to their terracotta-tiled house in Encino, along with their doggy bag of leftover New York Strip, and they have sex with him in their bed on top of their white cotton sheets. They're coyly discreet about the condoms, rolling one onto him without a word while Jane's taupe-nude lipstick smears across his mouth, no big deal, because they don't know where he's been, which is fair enough because Bunny doesn't always remember where he's been either. Bunny goes in the middle, sandwiched between his friends-for-the-night, with him on top and her underneath. *Oh yeah, fuck me, just like that, harder, baby, right there.*

Rocking between them, it's Bunny's responsibility to keep pace, sinking back onto him and sliding forward into her. There's an art to it, to giving two people what they want at the same time, putting on the perfect show of debauchery for them, the flexibility it takes to get his legs spread just right and back arched smoothly, a pornographic pin-up from every single angle. And, if he's nothing else at all, Bunny is a pornographic *artist.* He shudders out a perfect moan.

Sunrise watches Bunny leave, with the doggy bag of New York Strip that John lets him take home after he turns down the smoothie spinning around their Nutribullet. He waits for a bus and smokes a cigarette. They gave him money for a cab, but he likes taking the bus, likes being seen the morning after in the same clothes as the night before. The bus only gets him as far as Universal City and, from there, he hitchhikes back to West

Hollywood, thumbing a lift from a group of UCLA girls in their sensible-but-fun blue Prius on their way to a 9AM class.

One of them, the one who's pressed against his side as he squeezes into the back seat, gives him her number when they go out of their way to drop him off at his own car, still where he left it in the theater parking lot shared with the liquor store next-door. She's cute, like a certain type of girl in the movies he watches, fawning over his blond halo and the firm line of his bicep. "You could totally be a model," she suggests, and he knows she's just gagging for a gay boyfriend.

He loses her number amongst the Wendy's wrappers and CVS receipts in the footwell of his Cadillac.

It takes a couple weeks of dates—and they *must* be dates because John and Jane aren't paying him in anything other than dinners and cab fare—bouncing between bars and restaurants and their bed, before they bring up this idea they have. "*So, we were wondering,*" they say, "*if you'd be interested in trying something a little... different.*" They warn him that it might seem extreme, that they're prepared for him to say no, that they know not everyone would be up to it.

They already know Bunny will do it; Bunny doesn't say no to anything. Even so, the offer surprises him. While Bunny isn't into much of anything, he's still seen more than his fair share of dirty movies, had more than his fair share of eccentric hook ups, and done much more than his fair share of posing for the type of magazines he can't send home to his parents and are only found behind crusty black-velvet curtains. He knows what people get their rocks off to, and he knows that the "freaky shit" that John and Jane do to him three nights a week is nothing more than conversation fodder.

An experimental phase that they can brag about to their white-bread friends over brunch or during spin class, that will elicit a murmur of awe at how open-minded they are to unconventional pleasure. Something so unconventional that they had to cruise WeHo on a Monday night to find Bunny, the person they're told is freaky enough to be their deceased third.

But, in practice, they are as vanilla as it comes: a hesitant hand on his throat to choke him, never hard enough to bruise; the spankings that sting his ripe ass cheek, inflicted with the paddle he brought from home, the one with his own name embossed in mirrored letters, and that prompts a pantomimed moan each time Jane swings it; their curated selection of fresh-out-the-box sex toys that he lets them test out on him, watching him like a YouTube tutorial from the end of the bed while he lubes up a jeweled plug for them; making a guessing-game out of whether he's wearing a jock or panties beneath his jeans and the blush that spreads down both their necks when he bends down and shows them the answer; the sessions when he lets John practice his clumsy *shibari* with fresh red ropes crisscrossing Bunny's tanned chest, looping around his groin, the gag in his mouth making him drool, and leaving him with nothing to do but sigh and twitch beneath his soft hands, hoping that might make him pull his ropes tighter.

Hell, they wine-and-dine him for weeks before getting down to business, even though Jimmy must have told them what Bunny is willing to do, what he's willingly done, for far less. Agreeing to lie back and just let himself get fucked is the least kinky thing Bunny has done this week.

They fill the bathtub for him before he arrives, with cold water from the faucet and bags of cocktail ice cubes from Wholefoods, letting him sit there for too long, until he's so cold that he doesn't even shiver anymore. The first time he did it, he kind of felt like a salmon, presented alongside its catch-mates in a tub of ice at the fish market he went to with his Daddy back in Jacksonville.

Tense all over once he finally climbs out of the tub, Bunny bends over the bathroom counter, between the his-and-her basins and, with stiff fingers slippery with K-Y, he makes his insides as cold as his outsides with an ice cube shoved up himself. He's almost winded by the intrusion, sucking in a desperate breath as his left knee half-buckles beneath him. *Holy. Fuck.*

Bunny thinks about suggesting they take up community theater as a hobby, once they get bored of having three-ways, as he listens to their roleplaying. They act out finding Bunny dead in their bed and, despite the awful circumstances, they just can't help but notice that he's still absolutely *irresistible*. If they really want to spice up their sex lives, Bunny thinks they should host a murder mystery sex party, where everyone gets some alone time with the body to mourn his tragic passing, or to look for clues, or to do whatever they want and blame it on the madness of grief. That'd tickle their suburban sensibilities.

All the specifics of his demise are left vague, of course, but Bunny assumes it's nothing too gruesome. In Bunny's mind, it's an erotic-asphyxiation accident that takes him out—just the way god intended.

Playing dead is easy-peasy. The only thing he has to do is make sure his boner lasts against the odds of his wandering mind and dropping body temperature. The rest of it comes naturally to him: lying there quietly and doing nothing, arms and legs limp, eyes hazy. He's always been told so. Bunny's surprised by how close he comes to enjoying it.

Years ago, back before he learnt how to pose and pout, how to arch his back and bat his dark lashes, how to grab his own ass and flex his muscles in all the right ways, he'd been an easy yet terribly *boring* lay. Teenage escapades had been strange and fumbling experiences that never did much for Bunny. Hands that weren't his own on his skin, knowing they shouldn't be there but feeling them grab at him anyway, the emptiness in his stomach when he tried to focus on finishing, the unpleasantness of feeling so full that he just didn't know what to do, other than stay completely still and hope it passed soon.

The uncomfortable squeeze of something hot and wet around him, the sudden feeling of being a stranger who was merely inhabiting the body that they all called "Bunny." *It felt like nothing at all.*

Is this really what drives people crazy, what makes people cheat, and what started ancient wars? Because people couldn't get enough of this?

"You like that?" his girlfriend, Eloise, asked. She was on top, in the back of her dad's Toyota, outside a house party that had about 20 more minutes before it got broken up by the cops.

"Yeah, s'real good," he answered, grimacing at how tight she was on him.

"You're not actin' like it's good, Bunny," she said. "You never act like it's good."

Bunny gripped her hips harder, pressed a kiss to her sweaty neck and apologized. Just as the cops pulled up, Bunny finally managed to get her over the finish line, so at least he didn't feel too bad when they scrambled out of the back seat and he drove Eloise home.

A week or so later, on the sagging cord couch in their basement, Eloise's brother pulled out and finished all over Bunny's thighs. "It's like fuckin' a dead fish with you, Bunny," he said as he tossed Bunny his underwear a little meaner than needed.

Bunny thought about those fish, in their tubs of ice at the market he went to with Daddy on Sunday mornings, and he apologized. A football game played on the fuzzy, outdated TV set, the crowd roaring at a touchdown as Bunny pulled his clothes back on. He knew he better leave before Eloise got home from cheer practice.

Being dead clearly wouldn't change much for Bunny in terms of his fuckability. Under the most ideal of circumstances, he figures there's a certain sweet spot when he'd be at his prime, when he'd be at his most perfect: so *unresisting*, so easy to *defile*, but, most importantly, still *pretty*. If he was in a morgue, and they only rolled the slab out when someone wanted him, then he could last like that for a week, maybe, before he started to bloat and his insides leaked their way out of him. A chest-freezer would keep him pretty, sure, but it'd be so *impractical*. It's not like he could be thawed out more than once before the rot started to set in. Bunny watched an episode of *Law & Order* once where it took days for a body to completely thaw out. Not ideal.

After that, all hope would be lost for him. Freshly dead, Bunny could be almost angelic. Sure, he might be cold, his lips blue the same way they are after sucking on a blue raspberry Dum Dum—and isn't that an idea, maybe he should remember that trick for next time—but he would still be *perfect*. Waxed and tanned and bleached all over. That's all that matters.

A couple of days, weeks, months go by, however, and his pretty face will be gone for good. God, that really would be the end of him. John and Jane want to fuck him cold and unfeeling. Decomposing would be a step too far over the line of "experimentation." Decomposition would eat away at his peachy keen skin, turn it to sludge beneath Jane's fresh French-tips. They couldn't get all that mess all over their white-cotton bedsheets.

And that's assuming his death is pretty at all. That erotic-asphyxiation accident he's jonesing for, it would leave him with a storm cloud of bruises around his neck but otherwise photo-ready. No, Bunny will probably die in a pool of his own vomit somewhere, maybe in Jimmy's apartment in Malibu, or an alley off Sunset after he's been kicked out of the bar for the night, or in some motel on the city limits where they wouldn't be recognized. Skin-slip distorting his photogenic features, mottled purple and green and all the hues of death, decaying until he's nothing but bones and maggots.

One afternoon, while Daddy was cooking up the fish that they'd bought from the market that morning, Bunny, who had been sent to play outside instead of spending all his time watching them *damn videos*, found a dead rabbit in the scrub behind the house. It must have been there for a week or two already, with blowflies crawling where its eyes once were, clustered around where the purge had leaked from its mouth and ears and holes. Bunny poked the thing with a stick. There was nothing left of the rabbit, not at all, it was only being used as feed for the things that were living inside it now.

Shit, he's gonna lose his boner. Sometimes a change in position helps; he needs John to roll him over, Jane to prod at his soft spots, something to let his mind come back to his body for a minute, so he can think his cock back to hardness and then drift off again, thinking about the movies he's missing at the porno theater tonight. He wonders if Tony is missing him.

Of course they wouldn't ever want to watch *Nekromantik* with him. There's only a handful of people in the theater, even less than usual, and Bunny settles into his favourite seat in the middle row, a can of cherry Coke sweating in one hand and a packet of Red Vines clutched in the other. A few stragglers looking to cruise wander in but promptly walk back out, figuring they'd rather chance it with the curb-crawlers than try to keep it up with a rotten corpse on screen.

Bunny looks over at the girl three seats to his right. Women don't come here very often, it's not really their crowd. Some who do are exhibitionists, and some just want to ogle and see the depravity for themselves. Then there are the girls who are brought there by their boyfriends as a test, to see them squirm, humiliated by the silver screen smut. Not that it matters to Bunny why they're there, why any of them are there—he's busy watching the movie.

But this one, the girl three seats to his right, has her denim mini skirt up around her hips, her hand working quickly between her legs, beneath her stripy Walmart value-pack panties. She catches Bunny watching her and smiles, heavy-lidded and daring.

Bunny pulls the crumpled cigarette packet from his jeans, smiles back at her with his perfect porn star smile and lights a smoke.

Author Bio

Twitter & Instagram: @alien_annabel

This is Annabel Costello's publishing debut! She is from Manchester, England, where she had an annoyingly ordinary childhood. Luckily, she went to university to study film and creative writing, which is where she encountered the terrible, taboo, transgressive influences of slashers, pornography, and down-and-dirty sleaze. After disappointing her professors, she now writes about unlikeable characters who are queer in all the wrong ways and for whom she harbors far too much sympathy.

When Costello isn't doing that, she spends her time trawling the archives for films that should only be watched in seedy picture houses at midnight. She's also working on a novella that gives Bunny the attention he's such a whore for.

Want to reach me?!
Find me here:
Twitter/x: slxtvxmit
Telegram: slxtvxmit
Instagram: Morguebabii

Dropboxes, Pictures, Videos
Findom, 1+1 personal chats!

Contact me DIRECTLY for content!
(I sell via Fansly for
those outside the US)

Save Me, 6ft Emma Stone Nazi Dominatrix

By Charlie Babbit

What it is, is...it's a kind of attention.

You have to be present in the moment with me in order to put me in my place. You HAVE to. And whatever that means for me is typically fine, as long as I'm getting the attention I need, from you, specifically. For example:

It's not that I have any particular interest in piss. I truly don't. But YOUR piss, maybe I do. If you aimed it at me and just me. Then I might be really, really interested.

Likewise, I can't say it feels good to slap my balls PER SE, but it does kind of do it for me when YOU'RE the one making me do it. Because you're doing it to ME. I don't necessarily like being hurt. But if YOU'RE the one hurting me, maybe that changes things a little.

Furthermore, I'm not actually gay. Not even a tiny bit. I'm so fucking 24/7 horned up for women that it causes problems in my actual life. BUT there is just something about the way the *word* rolls off your tongue when you call me a faggot that makes me get all swoony and weak-kneed. Maybe I'm a little gay for you, in a way. You get it.

Call me a faggot again.

Again.

I do know why I'm like this, it's not even difficult to nail down. I was born and, immediately, everything went completely sideways for me. I came out of my mother, was promptly taken to a different room in the hospital, and never saw her again. She was "too young to have a kid" (she wasn't) and her parents disapproved of the father anyway (they did, and with excellent reason). So, I was put up for adoption. It's just what you did in the late '70s, when your second-generation unmarried Irish-Catholic daughter came home, impregnated by a scummy Middle Eastern hippie hairdresser drug addict bass player from Chicago. You make that problem go the fuck on away to Hell, don't you, Paddy?

After that, I wound up in a foster home for the first six months of my life (much longer than necessary but the dad guy forgot to sign over his parental rights so, stuck in foster limbo, I was). From what I understand, they did the barest of bare minimums to keep me alive. I was fed, which I do appreciate. I had exactly one item of clothing, although my adoptive parents had to bring something for me to change into when they finally got me because the single hand-me-down onesie stayed with the last foster family.

Also, I couldn't move my legs when they came to get me because I was never picked up and, when they did pick me up, I screamed, because I wasn't used to being touched. Isn't that sad? A little baby who never met his mother and didn't like being touched. Everybody put some money in the tip jar for Sad Baby.

But so, I grew into a man who only wants to be touched, but on very specific terms, who has both a bottomless craving for female validation (the no-mother effect) and a general repulsion for normal modes of expressing love: physically and emotionally.

I want SOMETHING. I need SOMETHING. Desperately. But the normal stuff, it feels wrong. The weirder stuff, it feels safer. That I can handle. Love me, watch me shrivel up and hide. Spit on me, slap me, rub my nose in it, maybe I come alive a little. That, in a nutshell, is why I am like I am.

I want your attention. I want it more than anything. I want your attention more than I want to fuck. I want your attention more than I need to come. My dick is a secondary thought at best. I want the attention. Attention. ATTENTION.

And the abuse is a kind of attention. Degradation is attention. You have to look at me to do it. You can't be on the phone with someone else while standing over me, straddling my face, forcing me to eat you out at the same time. Well, actually, maybe you can. Put a pin in that.

If you can make me feel special, I don't care if its nice-special or mean-special. Make it so I'm the only other person on the planet for a few minutes and you can do literally anything you can think of to me.

Please. Test this out.

This isn't a Backpage post. It's a Bat-Signal.

Try me.

Author Bio

Twitter: @BroIsDeceased

Charlie Babbit is the fake name of a real person. He writes and deletes things at a breakneck pace on both his hilarious Twitter and Substack. He once put a record out on a small Scottish imprint label but he can't tell you the name of the band because it's too easy to look him up but, rest assured, it was a good album.

Babbit is currently trying to get high less but he's not taking it very seriously. Posting smutty or maybe not stories to his Substack? More so. Check it at https://CharlieBabbitt.substack.com/ and now https://substack.com/@BroisDeceased

eye spy

By Cody Sexton

As kids, our curiosity is boundless, leading us down paths we never could've imagined. And sometimes, those paths take us to places we can't unsee. This is the tale of one such adventure that left me scarred, bewildered, and maybe just a little bit wiser.

Picture this: a quiet town where nothing exciting ever happens. The only thrill was watching paint dry, and we all agreed that it had its charm. But when I stumbled upon that fateful gloryhole, my life went from shades of beige to neon pink in a matter of seconds.

It all began innocently enough, as most questionable escapades do. My buddy Zack and I were playing hooky from school because learning about the Pythagorean theorem was clearly not as enticing as chasing squirrels, examining dead bugs, or perusing pornography we found in the trash. We were on a mission to find treasure, adventure, or at least something shiny enough to make our day slightly less dull.

We wandered into the forgotten corner of the local park, where rusty swings creaked in the breeze and weeds threatened to overtake the sad excuse for a sandbox. Just as we were about to declare our quest a complete waste of time, there it was: a small, unassuming hole in the wall, situated at the edge of a bathroom. The hole was at crotch height, located on the outside wall behind the building, just below the window of a stall.

Now, any normal kid would've thought nothing of it. Probably just some odd design choice made by an architect with a peculiar taste in aesthetics, right?

Wrong.

Zack and I, being the precocious bastard scholars of our generation, decided this was a top-secret hideout for spies.

Yes, that's right. Spies. Don't ask how we jumped to that conclusion—it's the kind of thing that only makes sense in the warped minds of prepubescent boys.

With reckless abandon, we approached the hole, ready to exchange top-secret intel. But as we peered through, our eyes met something far more baffling than covert documents or concealed microphones.

It was...an eye.

A lone, piercing blue eye staring back at us as if we just interrupted its afternoon tea.

My heart raced as I glanced at Zack, who seemed equally dumbfounded. We quickly realized that this was not the realm of espionage, but something altogether different and weirdly intimate. It dawned on us that this was a gloryhole—a term that only grown-ups with hushed voices would mention, and even then, only after sending all the kids to bed.

The temptation to flee was strong, but curiosity has a way of chaining us to the most ludicrous situations. So, like two morbidly intrigued moths to a flame, we decided to investigate further. With a certain blend of trepidation and the determination that only kids can muster, we decided to become gloryhole sleuths.

To our horror—or perhaps it was awe—the eye moved.

It blinked, confirming that we were not, in fact, hallucinating from boredom-induced delirium.

Then, a voice echoed from the other side, crackling like an old radio with poor reception. Based on the tone, we guessed it was a middle-aged man, sounding oddly like our gym teacher. "Who's there?" the voice whispered, its tone a mix of suspicion and intrigue.

It was at that moment our epic quest for adventure morphed into a desperate desire to escape. In retrospect, the reasonable response would've been to run away screaming. Instead, we responded in hushed tones, introducing ourselves as Zack and Cody, detectives of the Whitesburg branch of a Top-Secret Spying Agency.

The voice on the other side chuckled—a sound that ricocheted between eerie and oddly welcoming. "Well, Detectives, how about a game of 20 Questions? You ask, and I'll answer."

I'm not sure why we agreed. Maybe it was the audacity of our audaciousness. Or perhaps, in some twisted way, we were captivated by the surreal nature of the situation. Whatever the reason, we dove headfirst into a verbal exchange with the unknown presence on the other side of the wall.

As bizarre as it sounds, that conversation felt like the most exciting thing to ever happen in our drab existence. We asked questions ranging from "What's your favorite color?" to "Have you ever met a celebrity?"

And shockingly, our anonymous companion answered them all with a mix of whimsy and honesty.

Hours passed in what felt like minutes and, as the sun dipped below the horizon, reality started to seep back in. It was as if a spell had been broken, and we suddenly remembered we were talking to a stranger through a gloryhole.

Our childhood innocence, already teetering on the brink, shattered like glass.

With a sense of urgency, we bid our newfound friend farewell, promising to meet again someday—a promise we never intended to keep.

As we walked away from that dilapidated bathroom, the absurdity of the situation hit us like bricks. We'd inadvertently stumbled upon a moment of connection that defied our understanding of the world.

Looking back, that gloryhole encounter was like a slapstick episode from a sitcom we didn't know we were starring in. It was a lesson in the unpredictability of life, the absurdity of childhood logic, and the sheer strangeness of human interaction.

And though we never spoke of it again, it surely remained etched in our memories—a bizarre footnote in the book of our lives, forever reminding us that, sometimes, even the most mundane moments can turn into something unexpectedly extraordinary.

Author Bio

Twitter: @SliceOfAnxiety   Site: AThinSliceOfAnxiety.com

Cody Sexton is managing editor for *A Thin Slice of Anxiety*, founder of Anxiety Press, and co-founder of Translucent Eyes Press. He is a prolific graphic artist (see *That Which Hell Promises*) and produces striking novelettes like *Too Numb To Cum, Stories Only A Mother Could Love, All The Sweet Prettiness of Life*, and *Too Many Things Came To Nothing*.

Sexton also helped curate and featured in *Anxious Nothings*, a beautiful, ironically erotic book of essays, illustrations, poetry, and fiction. He did the same with *Mirrors Reflecting Shadows*, a mixed-genre anthology supporting LGBTQ suicide prevention via The Trevor Project.

HOney Suckling

By Ryan Warrick

"They say no human being is perfect.
Probably the same applies to fruits, too."
Eating too many pineapples may cause these side-effects.
—an OnlyMyHealth blog.

August 2008, *Penthouse*

Problems in that part of the bedroom? Need to make a change and fast? Feel unworthy of love? First of all, it's nothing to be ashamed of. All guys face it sooner or later. Her wincing, her choking, her gagging. Gargling, "*Ew!*" at the top of her lungs, with tears in her eyes like she just ate fermented cow patty. It's completely natural. But listen, in my experience, it doesn't have to be this way. A little work, and I promise your sex life will totally one-eighty. Three-freaking-sixty. Promise. Take it from me—you won't even recognize it when it's all over.

Listen. Carefully.

Imagine your friend David's girlfriend always says he tastes like lukewarm hotdog water and blue cheese. Whereas your friend Nelson's girlfriend has a slightly different opinion, often complaining how Nelson tastes like taking a long slob off a stick of salami left out in the sun too long. Your own girlfriend, she flipflops a lot. Sometimes you're like root rot and sometimes you're like pond skink. But what she says most is that you taste like sticking a paper straw in a post-game jockstrap and sucking really hard.

The worst of you though is definitely *il capitano* of the group, Cubby Kirkland, whose girlfriend Shannon relentlessly insists he tastes like digging up some dead guy and going down on his corpse. This is likely because Cubby's favorite snack is to stack a whole can of sardines on a bed of pickles and mayo, brewing within him a pretty dang ripe dude-goo that always makes Shannon wince, and choke, and gag.

"Sometimes," Cubby says, "she does that half-open mouth thing cats do when they smell something bad."

So, like, what I'm trying to say is—and if you're really ready to listen—it's her critique that will launch a whole new kind of sex life for you.

Because, next thing you know, Shannon tells Cubby she's done. She says she's spent way too many afternoons in Cubby's smelly bedroom, kneeling at the foot of his bed, her mind always twitching over the same anxiety.

Which will happen first? Will your mom barge in and catch us? Or will you shoot your stinky rope in my mouth unannounced?

Suddenly, Shannon's got standards. Effectively, Shannon's putting her foot down—immediately. She's done sucking off Cubby's stupid corpse until he learns some respect. And do you blame her?

She says it's so bad that, almost always, she prefers the mom option.

And obviously, Cubby's heartbroken. Genuinely, Cubby's desperate. So, Cubby does what all good solution-seekers do: Google, Google, Google. But before he has a chance to do anything about it, you and David and Nelson hear the exact same thing from your girlfriends, and then there's an all-out coup.

"That's it," David's girlfriend says. "At least until you learn what a girl wants."

"But more than just what a gender wants," Nelson's girlfriend says, always the more liberally perspective. "Because no *person* should have to put up with this yuck."

"Maybe I loved you," yours says. "But Shannon and Jasmine and Amy are right. You guys really are just so totally yuck."

For real, you're thrown. Collectively, you're devastated. But then Cubby emerges from the depths of Reddit, a warning in one hand and a solution in the other.

"Drink too much, and side effects can include nausea, numbness of the mouth, tooth decay, abdominal pain and excessive bleeding," he says. "But they say it makes you taste good. Like really frickin' good."

Cubby waggles a can of Dole in your face, gargling sweet relief.

Next thing you know, at parties, David plunges a car key into a Dole can instead of a beer can, sometimes shot-gunning four or five good ones in a row. Whereas Nelson really likes the way it makes his mouth go numb after he eats a lot of it, so there he goes, chopping up two or three full fruits into little pizza-shaped slices, going down on a long, fibery lunch. And you're a half-and-half guy yourself, interested in the fruit and the juice you squeeze out of it, both of which must be equally effective.

But Cubby, probably the most dedicated of you all, know what he does? He goes and makes a beer bong out of a funnel that his dad uses to change car oil, taking that sweet, sweet crotch-caramelizer straight to the head.

Bottom line is, you want it fresh. Brands like Tropicana and Minute Maid add all that processed sugar, which will just make you taste more like fish farts, like dog breath, or worse—like you're rotting inside out. Buying Dole is a pretty solid choice, but honestly, probably the best you can do is homemade squeezed. Because, with homemade squeezed, they say you'll turn from corpse to honey in no time.

They say, from durian to dulce in less than a month.

But then Cubby comes out and says what everyone's thinking. *There's still too much risk.* Because, like, do you really want to give the girls final say?

Cubby reminds you that you're not working on a strike system here. "We've got one shot and one shot only," Cubby says, brow furrowed, his face red and flushed.

You're in his bedroom. You're sitting on the floor while Cubby sits on the end of his bed just above you. He's firing off concern after concern.

"If I don't deliver next time Shannon gives me a chance..." Cubby says. He uses the words "wince" and "choke" and "gag."

David stands up and sits next to Cubby, a sergeant buttering his captain's onion. "And if Jasmine runs to the sink and spits me out all over the drain next time," David says, "then I can pretty much kiss love goodbye."

Nelson joins them. "And if Amy goes and hocks me into the carpet again," he says, "then I know for sure we'll never get married and have kids."

And of course you have to agree. The logic is just too sound. None of you will be worthy of love until you are fixed, until you are sweet. So, you stand up and say, "Sure." You say, "One shot and one shot only, kids."

Cubby nods, pride and glory glistening in his eyes.

Here's what you do:

Steal a few of those wooden stirring sticks from Starbucks. Twice a week, wipe one across your sock or Kleenex in a twirling fashion to collect a nice, generous sample. Watch it glob stringily to the stick's cheap wood, like honey. Then simply lick up and across, and *wallah*—all the data you need to ensure your girlfriend doesn't take your eye out with a rueful loogie next time she gives you a chance.

All the data you need for love.

And next thing you know, David reports some near-creamsicle results. Whereas our boy Nelson describes notes of brown sugar, supposedly putting down straight-up snickerdoodle. As for you yourself and me: watch in utter delight as you creep right past stevia, just a few notes away from your grandmother's famous simple syrup.

But Cubby? Cubby's gone crazy. Because now Cubby's the one who's got standards. Everyone is doing their damnedest to make boy-o proud, but he just never believes you. Everyone shoots off top-notch results left and right, and still, it's not enough.

You're in Cubby's bedroom again when he erupts from a long silence. He's been pouting all day. He's been acting out. The group reports they're getting sweeter all the time, covering a complete spectrum of flavor, something the girls will really love and, in turn, love you back, but Cubby just doesn't listen. He keeps calling you faggots and queers. Then finally his red, wrinkled face—consistently glazed in sweaty fury and frustration the last month—it suddenly pops. "Fine," Cubby says. "If you're *so sure*."

He yanks open his bedside table drawer and presents a box of Kleenex. He takes his phone out of his pocket, clickity-clacks something into it and all but hurls PornHub into the middle of the room. He says you are absolutely not working on a strike system here. He says you've got one shot and one shot only. He looks you dead in the eye, unzips his jeans and says it.

Cubby says, "Put your honey where your mouth is."

And so next thing you know, Nelson is bobbing his head in semi-satisfaction, saying how David really *does* taste like mango sticky rice, but just a bit too much hint of the sea.

"Almost there, bro," Nelson says.

Sampling Nelson, David gets defensive. David says that if Nelson thinks he's anywhere near bananas foster, then he's fucking crazy.

This harsh critique makes Nelson's lip get all big and pouty, so you push David's inconsiderate ass hard against the wall, waggle your finger in his face and say, "HEY, DAVID, NELSON TASTES GREAT!"

There's some disagreement about whether you're more pistachio or more Lipton tea. Except, how can these fucktards not see? You're goshdamn apple pie. You're tres leches and Turkish delight.

But once again, probably the most impressive of you is the man, the myth, the legend here. Because all three of you unanimously agree that Cubby's daily jug of homemade squeezed has *more* than detoxed him of all those sardines and pickles and mayo. Cubby is a bona fide piña colada in a hammock on an eternal vacation to Waikiki. One sip of the Cubster and you can feel the sweet island breeze wrap wistfully around your ankles, up across your nipples, and straight to your head.

Like, wow.

And well, next thing you know, Shannon's mascara is running. Cubby's day finally comes. The ultimate test.

And well, he wins. In fact, he wins a little bit too hard.

He uses the words "vacuum cleaner" and "pneumatic tube," and "rash." "The gurgling sound an automatic pool sweeper makes when it hits the surface a little too fast." Cubby says he's at four jugs of homemade squeezed a day just to keep up.

You can't believe it. David and Nelson worry. Cubby sucks it down as fast as Shannon sucks it out of him. It's impressive. It's insane. It's off regiment and it's the best thing you've ever heard in your entire life.

But then something starts happening. And, at first, everyone's like, it's probably nothing. Probably just imaginations run rampant. Probably just the result of too much fiber. Probably just too much sugar in the veins. Probably just classic paranoia. But not too long after Cubby and Shannon get whisked away on an infinite flow of Cubby's sweat, something kind of weird starts happening. But again, it's probably nothing.

Shannon slips and cuts herself chopping fruit one day, and the blood just comes and comes. Supposedly, the same thing happens when she nicks her leg shaving and she has to stand in the tub for like an hour 'til it finally clots. Plucking a hangnail off her pinky finger a few days later, the tiny laceration beads until it trickles until it pours.

"I had to double wrap it with fat rags just to make it stop," Cubby says.

And of course, the doctors just say bullshit. They say shit to her like, "You have to stop eating so much pineapple, Misses Cubby's Girlfriend."

And when Shannon says it's not her with the pineapple, that it's her boyfriend with the pineapple, that they have her confused with someone else, they don't believe her.

They call her a liar. They say the proof is most definitely in the pudding. They spin a bunch of bull about how certain foods affect blood, pointing to charts and waggling their fingers in her face, and never once do they relent in their belief that somehow, some way, the pineapple is getting into her from somewhere.

Cubby says Shannon left the appointment in tears, her mascara running all the way home.

And sure, there's that list of side effects that might bring a few things to light, reveal a diagnosis or two, but what do doctors know? What do doctors know about anything at all? *Shannon is not the one with the pineapple here.* Blaming it on the fruit, on Cubby's genius, is a low blow. And besides, everybody knows things like this resolve themselves. They always do. Shannon is a strong girl and, whatever is going on with her, she'll recover from it in no time.

It's not you. It's not Cubby. It's not the fruit.

How could it be?

And besides, today is no day for worry. Because today everyone is invited to Cubby's family's famous 4th of July BBQ, Shannon and David and Nelson and you, and look—everybody is in the pool.

Cubby's little brother is swimming in the deep end when a pink-tinged spray explodes from his snorkel. "I taste red slurpy," he says.

Cubby's mom, big floppy hat bobbing in an inner tube, asks if somebody spilled strawberry piña colada. She tells you to be more careful.

Cubby's dad, lounging in a submersible chair on the Shamu step, he gets a face-full of his youngest son's pink-tinged spray, prompting Dad to ask if that's coconut he's tasting, or maybe a new kind of Kool-Aid?

Something that looks like stained pineapple chunks bob downstream. Something red and gunky. Something slurry yet grainy, like chamoy sauce. It's the same color as when somebody at the beach shouts, "shark, for real!" but the smell is like the inside of a Jamba Juice. A sweet island breeze.

And, when you think about it, it's probably good that Shannon isn't really conscious enough to experience the mortification. Because, just moments after the smell completes its waft across the pool, is when they trace the plume back to her. It's a red dye twisting and tumbling like a magnificent underwater ballet between her legs, and they discover Shannon floating face-down in the shallow end.

Cubby swims over to her all crazy, desperately flailing his arms like Moses parting the Red Sea. He shouts for his dad to come help.

David says it's exactly like how your mom always warns, "Everything in moderation," whereas Nelson says they should've known to watch out for spiders hiding in the honeysuckle. Because, to your surprise, it turns out that pineapple is an excellent blood thinner, that it boosts red and white blood cell generation like crazy, and, in girlfriends like Shannon, can soften the uterine wall to the point of a way early and super intense flow.

But even though David and Nelson agree that somebody needs to speak up about what his little brother found bobbing in the deep end after Cubby and Shannon left in the ambulance... what Cubby's dad had to fish out with the pool skimmer... what barely had a face and at least eight webbed toes... what Cubby's dad says nobody can ever mention to Cubby's mom... Even though they say it's the right thing to do, you're whole-heartedly against telling him.

Because you're not done yet. Because you just know it'll throw Cubby off his game. Because there's a little more work to do before this is all said and done. Because, look. Because last week your girlfriend gave you your second chance, and know what happened?

She winced and she choked and she gagged. She did that half-open mouth thing cats do when they smell something bad. But guess what. You don't even care. Because, if anything, all of this makes you realize that there were girlfriends before her and there will be girlfriends after her. It's the stale, stinking, absolute sureness of life. Soon, life will come find you and it will give you a job and a house and a wife who hates the way you taste. But right now, you've got something you'll never have again. You've got something that, for the first time in your entire stupid existence, actually means something. You've got something to work towards that no one else has. You and Cubby and David and Nelson—chasing that sweet island breeze.

So, you really want to change your sex life? Really want to mix things up? Well, just imagine. Imagine you're walking into the hospital. You intercept Cubby and tell him what's what. You tell him, "We're not working on a strike system here." You tell him, "We've got one shot and one shot only." You tell him how it makes you taste good, like really freaking good.

Then you get on your knees, a jug of homemade squeezed in one hand and a funnel in the other, and you look Cubby dead in his eye and say it.

You say, "Put your honey where my mouth is."

Author Bio

Substack: https://RyanWarrick.substack.com/

Ryan Warrick likes to hide notes for strangers in unexpected places and wonders why nature has pretty much decided against blonde raccoons. When he's not out there trying to spot a blonde raccoon, he's either writing freelance web copy or writing fiction for friends, family, and strangers. His writing usually consists of yucky and/or unfortunate events, which he tries to end with some kind of wedding, baptism, or epiphany.

Warrick's Substack, *The Daily Lotion*, is free to subscribe. Readers can expect one to two stories a month, conveniently dropped into their email inbox or accessible via the Substack app/website. Additionally, you can find his work at *Propagule Magazine* and *Jersey Devil Press.*

Cog Fuck

By Neda Aria

Every weekday in Pedro's life followed a routine. Until the Monday that changed everything. Since then, every weekend has been spent fantasizing about the following week.

The alarm buzzed at 5:30AM, slicing through the predawn silence of his modest apartment. He lay in bed, eyes fixed on the ceiling, as the dull throb of the factory's machinery echoed in his mind. His wife's still form next to him. Her presence, more shadow than substance, barely registered in his mind. He swung his legs off the bed. With a routine that mirrored the methodical operations he supervised, he shuffled to the bathroom.

The fluorescent light flickered to life with a reluctant hum and a harsh white glow over the small room. He faced the mirror, the reflection gazing back at him: worn and perpetually tired. He checked if he needed to shave his stubble or if he should go to the barbershop as he brushed his fingers through his thick, wavy hair that seemed a touch too long. Then he squeezed a modest amount of toothpaste onto his brush, the stripes perfectly centered across the bristles.

The sound of brushing was rhythmic, a metronome to his half-awake senses. He counted each stroke as if tallying the minutes left until he must surrender to the factory's embrace. Rinse, spit, the swirl of water spiraling down the drain. Next came the shave. The razor glided over his stubble. With each pass of the blade, he imagined peeling away more than just stubble—stripping down layers, exposing the raw, hidden parts of himself that no one saw. He pressed a bit too hard on purpose, nicking his cheek.

Blood clumped with the shaving foam and hair, giving him a strange satisfaction as they dropped into the sink. A foreign trace of his existence washed away with a turn of the tap. The shower was brief and functional: soap, shampoo, rinse—the actions ticked off like a checklist.

Dressed in his work uniform, each button fastened, each crease aligned, Pedro went to the kitchen and prepared his usual breakfast: two slices of toasted bread, a dollop of butter, and a cup of black coffee. He ate in silence, the only sounds being the crunch of toast and the soft slurp of coffee. By the time the clock struck 6:15, Pedro kissed his still-asleep wife goodbye, locked the apartment door, and left.

The city was beginning to stir, and the bus ride was a blur of drowsy faces and muffled sounds. The factory loomed ahead, its towering smokestacks belching white smoke into the dawn sky. As he stepped through the gates, the familiar discord of the heavy machinery welcomed him—an orchestra of metallic clicks, steam hisses, and sharp clanks. Pedro smiled. He felt as if he belonged here as much as all the machines. It made him giddy. Outside, he felt foreign. Here, he was somebody, and everything was predictable: inspecting gears, adjusting pressures, ensuring safety protocols.

Evening came as a shadow, slow and stealthy. The factory whistle signaled the end of the day and Pedro joined the queue for his daily wage—a line of workers winding through the corridor like a trail of weary ants. The anticipation of receiving his pay stirred a perverse pleasure in him, an erotic charge pulsating through the mundane act of waiting. That is why, he always waited at the very end of the line. Every day at this time, he envisioned himself as a prostitute, collecting his night's earnings from a pimp. The tattered bills felt sensual in his hands. He savored the tactile sensation and its odor that reminded him of semen, a raw, primal smell that was both repulsive and salacious. The transaction was swift, impersonal, yet for Pedro it was a small, secret thrill—a dirty reward for his day's toil.

The factory's din faded just like Pedro's smile when he made his way home: the same steps retraced, the same scenes replayed. His wife sat in front of the TV, the plate of usual spaghetti in hand, her figure barely moving, immersed in the show she was watching. He sat beside her, grabbed his plate, and ate silently. Bedtime marked the conclusion of his daily ritual. At 9:30PM: brushed teeth, checked locks, lights off. In the quiet darkness, he lay awake beside his wife, who, after a perfunctory goodnight kiss, turned her back to him and dropped into a deep sleep.

The silence was absolute. The factory's clicks, hisses, and clanks echoed in his head, perfectly synchronized with the jerks of his left leg. These spasms were both irritating and persistent. They happened like any other routine in his life, just as he was about to fall asleep. Despite reassurances from doctors that it was normal and nothing to worry about, he couldn't simply disregard them. With each involuntary movement, a numbing itch would burn deep within his bone marrow. They would persist unless he played with himself.

Every jerk of the leg would fade with every stroke of his hand in bizarre synchronization with the factory sounds in his head. It was like Beethoven's "Symphony No. 5" playing:

Click.   Hiss.   Clank.
Click.   Hiss.   Clank.
Click. Hiss. Claaaaaaank.

Each movement was mechanical, devoid of thought, as if his body knew the routine by heart and his mind was merely a spectator. After orgasm, he fell asleep. It was every day of Pedro's life and weekends spent fantasizing about Monday. But that Monday, everything changed.

The factory was buzzing with activity. Pedro walked through his routines with an almost religious zeal. Each motion was meticulously executed, each check marked with obsessive care. Midway through, a harrowing scream shattered the mechanical harmony, slicing through the clatter like a fart at a formal dinner party. His heart stuttered. He whirled around and saw a cluster of workers, their faces drained of color, forming a tight circle, murmuring in panic. Running toward them, his boots ominously squeaked on the slick floor.

Breaking through the crowd, he saw Martin, a new trainee, clutching the stump where his hand had been. Blood splattered the floor, pooling darkly under his severed wrist. Martin's face was ghostly pale, his eyes wide with shock and agony as he shuddered, futilely trying to grasp the hand that had been cleanly cut off by the machine's blades.

Instinctively, Pedro barked orders for the emergency shutdown and called an ambulance. A ghastly silence filled the factory as the machines jolted to a stop. He kneeled by Martin, took off his jacket, and pressed it against the wound, the fabric quickly soaking with blood, trying desperately to slow down the flow until help arrived.

After the paramedics whisked Martin away, Pedro remained there, motionless, the bloody jacket clutched in his trembling hand. The factory resumed its noisy bustle, supervisors shouting instructions, workers whispering in hushed, horrified tones but, to Pedro, it was all a distant buzz.

That night, sleep became a stranger. Pedro lay wide-eyed. The accident played endlessly in his mind. It was not guilt that gnawed at him for overlooking his work duties, but a morbid curiosity about the machine that effortlessly mutilated Martin. It was as if it bared its sinister soul to him, like a demon, tempting him, calling him, wanting *him* bare to the bones.

A perverse longing to understand—to perhaps even *feel*—the icy caress of those merciless cutters made him hard. This time, he beat off like the Brahms' "Symphony No. 1":

Stroke.   Stroke.   Stroke.   Long stroke.

Stroke.   Stroke.   Stroke.   Long stroke.

Stroke. Stroke. Stroke. Loooooooooong stroke.

He stroked so hard and came with a moan so loud that it woke his wife. And from that night, each night, as his wife's steady breathing filled the space, Pedro imagined the steel blades of the machine instead of his restless leg. And he jerked off as never before. And he came as never before. Gradually, this trance seeped into his daytime routines.

At work, he found himself standing longer than necessary before that very machine, studying its mechanics, its precise and unforgiving nature. He began to personify it, seeing it not as an instrument, but as a thing that made his orgasms meaningful—a sacred calling for self-amputation.

As days bled into weeks, his daytime activities became mere intermissions to the relentless theater of his dark thoughts. At work, he kept a detached, almost scholarly interest in the mechanics of the machinery, but, at home, his research took a more morbid turn. He scoured the internet for medical articles on amputation. He searched for doctors who might discuss elective amputation, but each inquiry was met with stunned silence or curt refusals. The medical community could not—would not—entertain his spiraling desires and, if they would, he couldn't afford the price.

His desperation mounted after a month of searching for an answer. Every closed door only served to intensify his fixation. The lack of real answers and the absence of a path forward, twisted his obsession into something gnarly and pervasive. One morning, while shaving, he stared at the blade in his hand, wondering what would happen if he pressed a little harder, moved a bit closer, and sliced—not just the stubble, but—the very tip of his nose or maybe his tongue. He shuddered at the thought yet couldn't dismiss it.

Later, while spreading butter on a slice of toast, he fantasized about the knife carving into his thumb. He imagined the clean cut, the sudden shock of pain, the bright blood—a preview of the liberation he believed would come with greater sacrifice.

That day, work passed in a blur. All he remembered was the blade of the machine and the compulsive thought of cutting himself. He came home early, finding his wife peeling potatoes for dinner. He stood there, wrestling with the idea of confiding in her. He imagined starting the conversation with, "Can we talk?" to which she'd reply, "About what?"

He'd say, "I've been having these thoughts...about an accident at work. A trainee cut his hand in a machine."

She'd say, "What about it?"

He'd say, "I think it evoked a craving. I want to cut my leg."

She'd sigh and say, "You're just stressed, Pedro. Don't think about it so much."

He thought, if he talks, she would hear him, yes, but she wouldn't listen, not really.

So, he remained silent, watching her peel.

He looked pale and parched; his gaze fixed on her hands. The way the peeler stripped the skin away in smooth curls fascinated him: the simplicity and efficiency of it. *This is it*, he thought.

After his wife fell asleep that night, he went to the kitchen and took the peeler in his trembling hand. He stood by the sink, rolled up his sleeve, his heart pounding in his ears, the metal cold and menacing against his forearm. With a mix of dread and arousal, he began to peel, the pain sharp and immediate.

He hissed.

The tool fell off his hand.

Blood dripped fast. Tears welled in his eyes—not from the pain or regret but out of joy.

Of how hard and alive it made him feel. The thin strip of skin and fat felt as foreign to him as his left leg below the knee. He made up his mind.

Friday, he would give in to the machine.

Friday had always brought a certain relief around the factory, a collective exhalation as the week's labors wound down, but it was never the case for Pedro. The thought of leaving the factory for two whole days was once merely daunting; now, it was utterly intolerable. And this Friday was a crucible of his own making. He was painfully aware of each ticking second, each heartbeat in his chest as he yearned to linger by the machine.

Around him, his coworkers chatted idly about weekend plans. Pedro kept glancing towards the foreman, a gnawing suspicion in his gut that someone might notice his loitering, might question his fascination with the machinery. His visits to the site of Martin's accident had become more frequent, his inspections unnecessarily thorough, and some told him this was bordering on obsessive.

He needed to be near it, hear its whisper, and feel its cold, metallic touch. Yet he couldn't stay without raising suspicions, without risking questions he couldn't answer. The stress of maintaining a façade of normalcy while his mind roiled with dark desires was eating him from within. As he clocked out, he threw a last, longing look over his shoulder at it. His footsteps hollowly echoed in the emptying parking lot, a sound too loud in the quiet desperation of his departure.

He hid in the emergency stairways of the parking lot until night arrived. When the sound of traffic subsidized and the crickets began chirping, he returned to the factory.

The building stood silent—a cathedral of steel where Pedro sought his twisted salvation. The clock struck midnight as he entered through the side gate, the security lights casting long, eerie shadows that danced along the walls like ghosts. Inside, the air was thick with oil. His footsteps echoed in the space, his heart pounding in sync with the throbbing of his hard cock.

He approached the machine. Its blades faintly gleamed in the dim light.

He caressed the machine as if he was touching the naked body of a lover. In this quiet, sacred moment, his mind reeled with the visions that had haunted him: his limb, severed and sacrificed, an ultimate orgasm mixing his sperm with the blood. He trembled. He imagined the clean slice, the sudden liberation, the finality of it all—to get rid of his leg, which felt too foreign to belong to his body. An extra piece of meat and bone he never felt was part of him.

He removed his clothes and positioned his leg just within reach of the mechanism. The temptation to activate the machine whispered to him, a siren call that was both terrifying and seductive. His hand hovered over the control panel, the metal buttons cold beneath his fingers. He steadied his shaky breath and pressed the button.

The machine roared to life, the blades spinning with a terrifying precision.

The blade met his flesh.

A searing pain exploded through him, more intense than anything he had imagined.

The world blurred into a whirl of light and sound, his screams lost in the noise of the machinery.

Overwhelmed by pain, blood loss, and orgasm, his consciousness flickered and then went dark.

The next thing he knew, he was blinking against the sterile brightness of a hospital room, confusion muddling his thoughts.

A nurse was beside him. She smiled at him. "How are you feeling?" she asked softly.

Pedro swallowed, his throat parched, "Thirsty."

She handed him a cup of water, which he gratefully sipped.

As reality slowly pieced itself back together, a troubling thought surfaced. "Did... Did something happen to me?"

The nurse's smile faded as she replied, "When they brought you in, it was too late. Unfortunately, the doctors couldn't reattach it."

Pedro's heart sank as he processed her words. He lay back. He felt a weight off his shoulder. He tried to control his smile.

The nurse said, "You're lucky to be alive. It could have been much worse."

Pedro nodded.

She left.

He sighed with relief. His hands trembled as he grabbed the edge of the blanket to see what freedom looked like.

His heart pounded so fast as he slowly pulled the blanket.

It fell off the bed.

He choked on his saliva when he saw both legs intact.

His left leg jerked.

Author Bio

Twitter: @NedaAria   Instagram: @NedaAriaStories

Neda Aria, also writing under the pseudonym Lilith Wilde, is known for her explorations of subversive fiction, dystopian themes, and intense romance. Her most notable works include *ENARO, Feminomaniacs, and Machinocracy*. Under the name Lilith Wilde, she has published *Bella Donna*, and her upcoming novel *Red Wings*, the first in the Lust in Paris trilogy, is set to be released by Outcast Press in 2025.

Aria, in addition to her solo works, has hosted several collaborative anthology projects, *including DiverCity, Hikikomori,* and *Pixelated* (forthcoming), which feature diverse voices across transgressive and sci-fi genres.

More From Our Authors

Tina is chasing the American dream—the dream of escape, running from a life that never fits. From the crowded streets of '90s Iran, every step forward is a fight against tradition, family, and the limits she can't easily break. It's a story of growing up free when the world won't let you, of wanting more, and the bittersweet taste of finally getting it, even if a little, even if from a lost-in-life boy named Gus.

Counting Crows by Neda Aria is a literary duet with *Lover's Rock* by Aaron Paul Schaut. These two separate yet intertwined stories follow Tina and Gus through love, longing, and the echoes of a past they can't outrun. These books must cum together. We recommend you scissor them for a more pleasurable read.

Ladyboy

By Robb White

"Well, guys, that's it, another fun adventure completed. Hope you enjoyed our tour of Tokyo's adult zone. See you tomorrow. We'll check out more famous sites in the Shinjuku District... Until then, don't do what I wouldn't do!"

Shutting down vlogging was his favorite time of day, any day, anywhere—*Except*, he thought for the hundredth time, *there's very damn little I won't do.*

His internet handle was Happy Nomad. It took years to build up a following while hitchhiking on the backs of "motos," hiring tuk-tuks and rickshaws by hustlers who drove him everywhere but where he wanted to go and charged him twice as much; he'd piled into buses reeking of gabbling locals, squalling children, and enough body odor to gag a maggot. He'd survived on packages of ramen noodles in third-rate hotels for months, always smiling and joking for his fans over the rumbles of his stomach.

When money was short, he'd climb out of any hotel that didn't have bars on the windows to skip out on the bill. That got him a beating in Peru and almost cost him three years in a Havana prison until he bribed a national police officer to check out his travel papers with his last hundred dollars in his wallet.

He hadn't hit the jackpot yet—but he felt he was close. His cheap, scuffed GoPro stayed in his luggage while his new, expensive vlogging camera took over.

His reputation was everything to him. Every close call on the road pumped up his numbers. His most devoted followers spread his reputation internationally and often dared him to top his latest adventure with one even more daring.

Chandler Plett gave his sign-off with the usual body English his followers loved: He twisted his pelvis and lowered his spine in a corkscrew motion that ended with blowing a kiss to his audience. They emulated it when they passed him on the streets of London, Ecuador, Chile, or Baghdad. He reveled in his internet fame and when crowds gathered around, like that time in Bangladesh where dozens of children and adults followed him down the unpaved, winding streets of Dhaka churned to a red slurry by monsoon rains.

He never paid guides or locals to escort him. That was for chickenshits. If it meant being chased out of neighborhoods or down streets by rock-throwing thugs, so be it. The same thing could happen in D.C. or L.A. in the States.

He knew what it was like to be threatened by knives and clubs, and he had an instinct for distinguishing between men who *acted* tough and eyeballed him, and those quiet ones who'd glance at him passing by. Some gave off vibes you didn't test. He saw someone beaten unconscious in Brazil by a man at an outdoor stall who then calmly returned to his post to finish his Fernet con Coca.

Chandler still had nightmares of the Rocinha hillside slum in Rio. A mere mile from the beach, the favela sloped downhill after a thousand twists and turns; he was like a character buried alive in a Poe story. Instead of a coffin, he was trapped in a massive concrete maze with walls so narrow, his shoulders scraped the sides. Money and fame were his North Star and gyroscope that kept him on course and pointed him toward success, if he just stuck it out one more day, did one more video groveling for clicks, and held that phony smile pasted to his face until he thumbed the red light off.

Trekking through one shithole after another in 52 countries would one day pay off and make the dangers worthwhile. He once had his wallet stolen by a boy in Paraguay holding a gun way too big for his small hands. Black eyes and sprains from kicks thrown by neighborhood toughs only kept him coming back. He'd had the sneakers on his feet and the ballcaps on his head stolen. He'd been slashed with a knife once in Beirut. He rolled with punches, curled into a fetal position with his camera hugged to his belly to prevent them from stealing it.

Was it worth it?

Hell yes, it was worth it! 250,000 followers at last count. The number climbed after every misadventure in a red-light zone. Two major sponsors, a start-up sports drink company in L.A., and a major tool manufacturer with Home Depot distribution were emailing. Big fish smelled chum in the water, which meant the big money wasn't far behind.

Now this. God damn it.

He had just begun his first night of the Tokyo tour in the Kabukichō adult zone after scoping out places where he could find good trouble for YouTube posting—this, of course, after hours of editing, inserting music, and comical bits cut and pasted from his IMDb page to enhance the hijinks. While scouting, he ignored the fans who flagged him down for selfies or gave back his signature sign-off. Like that cutie in bangs down to her eyes in the sailor suit, pronouncing his line, "Do don't what I wouldn't do!"

He wanted to put the camera down and bone her against the nearest shop doorway. But, when he was on business, he was all business. The fun would come later, when the camera was off. Being a famous YouTuber had perks as well as obligations. He envied those internet influencers with their million-plus followers. He'd been paddling in the shallow end of the kiddie pool too long.

The phone call that afternoon, after he returned to his third-rate hotel, threatened to spoil everything. It came after he showered, sat on the bed, and took out the city map again for directions. The phone on the nightstand rang. A metallic voice, accentless, robotic—one of those voice scramblers: "There's a parcel outside your door, Mister Plett. Pick it up. I'll call back in five minutes." The connection ended.

There was a small package wrapped in plain brown paper tied with a string, his name on the front. No return address. A flash drive. No note.

The lens cut to an outside view of the city. He recognized Bangkok. Then a jump cut to the vibrant streets of a red-light district. Soi Cowboy. He knew all four from his walking tours. Another rough cut to a sleazy hotel from the street. Then a darkened interior of a basic room, the video shot from a pinhole camera opposite the bed. A supine male was being orally serviced by an energetic Thai hooker while a second girl, nude, fondled the stiff member for her companion.

Asian porn, what the hell. The stuff was free. He was blocks from one of the world's most famous red-light zones, the Kyakuhiki where girls with laminated cards advertised fellatio and hand jobs. Yoshiwara was closer, with the notorious "soaplands," where intercourse was negotiated between customers and "soap girls" in bathhouses-turned-brothels run by the Yakuza. He was about to shut down his computer when the dragon tattoo on the girl's shoulder struck a chord in his memory.

Oh shit. Not a pair of girls blowing a tourist in a cheap hotel. One prostitute and a ladyboy, Thailand's third gender. He recalled the night three years ago like an old VHS film skipping in its sprocket. He'd tramped up and down Patpong, Nana Plaza, and Soi Twilight until three in the morning, before bidding his followers good night with what would become his trademark farewell to the day's filming.

He was horny enough after scoping a million bar girls' asses and boobs. Resigned to accepting one of these hustlers, he spotted a freelancer at a nearby table: well-dressed, pretty, probably an office worker who needed more money than her salary to afford the latest iPhone. He was adept as any foreigner patrolling Thailand's Pattaya District for a better class of lay. With three Tiger beers under his belt, he began a conversation with her and, in minutes, they were discussing a price. She asked him if her girlfriend could join them. Chandler Junior made that call without hesitation—a twofer. Hell yes.

Just before the rocket went off, the ladyboy's Adam's apple became visible. Chandler wore a buzzcut in those days. But he couldn't change his face.

Ringtones from his cell on the night table.

He growled into the phone, "Who the fuck are you?"

The reply was curt: "You don't expect me to answer that, do you?"

"Get to it, asshole. How much?"

"No money, Mister Plett. It's simple. I'll ask you to perform three certain tasks and confirm them on your GoPro. I assume you still carry one. You used to. If you do these small exercises to my satisfaction, I'll send you the only other copy of the videotape."

"What kinds of small tasks—and how do I know you don't have more copies?"

"Trust, Happy Nomad. Trust. Our relationship will be based on mutual trust entirely, although if you fail to send me proof to the email address provided, I will expose you."

"You motherfucker! Fuck you! Upload the fucking video! See if I give a shit!"

The ladyboy film, however, worried him despite calling that scumbag's bluff. Hell, the room was dark, it would be easy to deny it was him. He couldn't be the only YouTube vlogger out there monetizing a gig unlucky enough to draw a lowlife scammer. But would a major sponsor touch his "product," as he considered his website, if there was even the whiff of scandal?

He couldn't be sure. The rumor might be enough to sink him. Followers who commented were often brutal in their remarks on his character.

"If that's your choice, very well," the scrambled voice replied.

"Wait! Hold on, jerkoff," Chandler said. "Give me the task and I'll decide whether I want to do it."

"Go up to the roof of your hotel and stand on the edge with a smoke bomb in your hand. Wave it about until the smoke is gone."

"That's it?"

"That's not quite it. One more thing. You have to be totally undressed."

You fucking asshole. Jesus, Mary and Joseph. Naked on a rooftop, waving a smoke bomb! Japanese laws were strict involving foreigners purchasing fireworks. But they were downright harsh when it came to foreigners weenie-wagging on rooftops. This was insane. He was doomed, doomed... His dream of making big money would fly off the roof the moment his foot stepped on the ledge.

His hand shook as he flung open the fridge door and grabbed the first bottle with alcohol and drained it in three gulps.

Later, calmer, he wondered whether it could be one of his rivals, a competitor, someone envious of his success. One of those dullards who got a haircut in a foreign country and believed they'd gone native. *Well, screw it. Let him put it up. I'll joke about it.* Trash streaming was becoming a thing, now big in Moscow. Pay some dude to do something violent or stupid and stream it live.

Buying fireworks in Japan was no problem in summer but as easy as taking a straight piss with Parkinson's at this time of year. The problem was solved, however, when he found a package containing a smoke bomb outside his door in the morning. The note inside was a single sentence in block print: **9PM facing Shibuya Crossing.**

You slimeball, thought of everything, have you? At least it's at night.

Getting access to the rooftop was the problem. He spent the morning and half the afternoon following staff until he located a maintenance worker who, for 50 dollars cash, agreed to give him brief access to the roof so that he could film a "panorama of Tokyo."

The man stepped back from Chandler's breath; he'd found liquid courage in the minibar fridge and guzzled everything alcoholic.

Once he was up there, he located the direction for Shibuya Crossing and began running toward it, stripping off his clothing as he aimed for the ledge.

The horrified maintenance worker ran after him, no doubt thinking he had a crazed suicide on his hands, yelling in rapid Japanese.

Chandler glanced backward, saw him fall to his knees, bawling on the asphalt roof. Chandler attached the GoPro band to his forehead, thumbed it on, and stepped up to the edge, risked a quick look down from that dizzying height.

With a fast pull on the ring, he ignited the bomb. Red smoke billowed out. The backwash of the wind blew smoke in his face, causing him to totter for a moment.

Only a telephoto lens could have captured the scene, but then, this was Japan. Sigma, Sony, Canon, Nikon—they came out of the womb looking for their mother's teat with an iPhone in one fist and an Android in the other.

Chandler didn't expect what happened.

His fear dissipated with the rising swirls of smoke. He found a thrill seeping into his belly and then, most unexpectedly, tumescence.

He was half-rigid by the time crowds below gathered in pockets at the intersection to gape in amazement at the bizarre sight of a nude man holding a smoke bomb.

Chandler began giggling. He was exhilarated, not ashamed at all. In fact, he hooted back at the people staring up at him. He gyrated, nearly losing his balance, to let his cock slap him in the stomach. He howled with glee.

With the last of the smoke dissipating, he jumped down from the ledge and raced to the old man, who fell to his haunches in terror at the crazy man running toward him.

Chandler hoisted him to his feet by his triceps and hustled him toward the stairway before cops came running.

They left the rooftop together. The exasperated man fired off a litany of what were no doubt curses at Chandler. By the time they returned to the top floor of the hotel, Chandler was less anxious but apprehensive about the threat of cops.

His giggling fit returned; he wondered if a cock photo taken from below would be enough to identify him. He stuffed all the yen and U.S. dollars in his wallet into the old man's hands for his silence.

Watching him flee down the hallway, clucking and bowing as he went, Chandler hoped he'd bought enough time to make his exit to a new hotel.

He sent the GoPro video to the email address the blackmailer had included with his note.

Chandler's room phone rang a half-hour later.

"Well done."

"Fuck you, jerk. Send me the flash drive."

"It'll be outside your door before morning."

And I'll be ready, motherfucker...

You can get a meal at Wolfgang Puck's restaurant or a McDonald's hamburger in Shinjuku. Buy any number of Pokémon figures, anime DVDs, or samurai collectibles. You'd have no trouble finding a bamboo walking stick at any number of stalls down there with a variety of handcrafted goods. Chandler picked one that made a pleasing whistling sound when he swung it around in a homerun strike.

Staying awake with caffeinated drinks and chewing CLIF bars until his jaws ached was the easy part. Not so easy was figuring out who the blackmailer could be. He ran through all the places in Thailand and Japan he'd been where he might have made an enemy. No viable candidates came to mind. He disregarded the petty stuff like beating a diner's check or taking a five-fingered discount at a market stand. His followers gleefully commented on his sticky-fingered artistry, although he told them he "always returned to pay back the money." Getting chased down the street by an angry shopkeeper meant bonus followers.

He held his pose, stick in hand behind the door, listening for any sound on the carpeting outside. He heard the muffled chattering drunks and giggling lovers go past until he couldn't keep his eyes open. He finally slumped to the floor with a bedsheet around his shoulders, confident he could spring into action and clobber the living shit out the bastard before he could escape down the hallway.

Around dawn, he heard clicking outside his door. He jumped to his feet and flung open the door.

A maid at her cleaning cart saw him with his cane upraised. She fled, screaming down the hall.

20 minutes later, the front desk clerk stood at his door with a frowning security guard behind him.

Chandler didn't need Japanese to know he'd been booted from the hotel.

He was in the street with his luggage in 15 minutes, entering an orange-checker taxi en route to his new hotel. *Problem solved.* The thought of someone tracking him from Bangkok had preyed on his mind more than he realized.

He was in luck that night with friendly crowds of locals and tourists. He downed a couple Sapporo beers in a bar with three attractive young females, none of whom spoke English, and spent a delicious five minutes chatting up a Scandinavian beauty with ample cleavage in front of Maison Margiela in the Shinjuku Station area. If her Viking of a husband hadn't been glaring at him the whole time, he'd have made a play for her digits. He arrived back at his hotel at 2:30 in the morning.

"Son of a bitch," he muttered.

Another small package lay in front of the door.

This flash drive created a bubble in his esophagus when he viewed it. It showed him talking to a young girl in downtown Bogotá—a notorious, filthy slum where prostitutes in miniskirts stood in open doorways up and down the blocks, soliciting without speaking a word unless approached. Chandler filmed the girls with a hidden camera, occasionally stopping to chat with someone in broken Spanish. The encounter was purely innocent, however.

He'd asked the girl how she came to the Colombian capital and wound up on the streets. He didn't give a shit about her; he wanted the human-interest element for his next posting: the Happy Nomad, a man with heart. His pidgin Spanish was altogether missing; her lengthy response deleted, all but the part where she spoke of using sex for survival. Chandler's voice was dubbed over by someone who also spoke poor Spanish. Instead of asking her questions about her pathetic life, the video was edited to make it sound as though he was asking the poor girl for sex and inquiring about prices.

Nothing sticks like mud. He could kiss those sponsors goodbye and say hello again to a minimum-wage job in Boise, right back to square one while carrying the stink of being exposed as a nasty perv to boot.

The flash drive came with a longer note: "I could choose to let you off easy this time. Setting fire to the hotel dumpster or maybe make you panhandle for loose change at busy intersections. But you, Chandler Plett, have such an ego that you need to be punished where it hurts most. Right in your inflated ego... Get this tattoo before 10AM tomorrow anywhere on your body or the video goes public."

The blackmailer listed five addresses, all legitimate, including his parents' back in Idaho. The rotten bastard had every email address from all of his emails, including the ones he used anonymously on his travels.

Chandler turned over the note and read his new tattoo: "I **Have a Small Dick**."

10AM—Jesus Christ.

It was three in the morning. Most shops didn't open until noon or later. Chandler bolted for the doorway and ran down the stairs to the lobby without waiting for an elevator. He flagged down a green taxi cab out front. Using hand gestures and waving a fifty-dollar bill at the cabbie, he finally made him comprehend that he wanted a tattoo parlor right away. The driver took him to a house in Shibuya with the shop located on the floor below.

It was closed.

Before Chandler could signal the taxi, the driver sped off, relieved to be freed from the crazed gaijin in his back seat. So, Chandler banged on the parlor door until a light came on in the room above. A young woman hollered down at him from an open window. She was the owner and the tattooist.

When he held up a fistful of hundred-dollar bills, she shut the window and came downstairs.

Chandler fell to his knees, begging her to tattoo him with similar hand gestures as he used with the cabbie. He grabbed her hand. Before she could pull it away, he stuffed three hundred-dollar bills into her small fist.

She held up a single forefinger. First, she pointed at him, and then pointed at her shop door.

He didn't understand what she said. He hoped it meant "one hour."

He sat on the curb with his head in his hands. His thoughts were murderous, bloody. The tattoo was no problem: He'd laser the damn thing off once he was back in the States. Before that, he'd show it to his adoring followers on a future videotaping, find some drunk in a no-frills tachinomi (standing) bar and make up a story about losing a bet—something to add luster to his bold reputation. The bigger worry was how to get revenge as soon as he was clear of this ongoing nightmare.

Chandler experienced what the Japanese call a satori: a revelation. He knew the blackmailer's identity in a flash of insight. The man was in his fifties—a Dutchman or a German, he recalled from the thick accent. An executive in the tech industry for some IT firm. He was one of those aging, desperate, pathetic men who patronize Thailand's billion-dollar sex industry. Chandler had interviewed him for the channel at a table beneath a colorful beach umbrella. The man spoke of his dual life in Europe and Thailand. Mostly, he talked about enjoying the companionship of a girl one-third his age, who was wading in the turquoise water offshore, smiling at them. Her thong accentuated all the right parts.

Chandler nodded along while the fatuous old fool droned on to his own humiliation. Chandler's commentators had a field day mocking him when he uploaded the episode.

Chandler recalled her easily because he bumped into her while she was shopping downtown. Her pot-bellied sugar daddy worked at his computer in the afternoons so Chandler seduced her, took her to his hotel, discreetly filmed their sex with a pinhole camera for his personal collection.

In an unusual moment of pique or mischief, he sent the tape to the man's hotel on the day he left for Japan. The guy irked him with his condescending attitude. He wrinkled his face when Chandler explained how he intended to make a career out of vlogging. That somehow rankled his working-class sensibilities. He wanted that snob to see his bought-and-paid-for woman really enjoying herself with a hard cock.

Dumb, fucking dumb...but too late now.

He was the only guy who had a grudge, the money, and the time to make Chandler's life miserable.

Aiko had no idea what the English words meant that she tattooed onto Chandler's right shoulder. The money wiped out her curiosity. Back at his hotel, he ripped away the bloody bandage and used the mirror to reflect the words he had to film. The digital clock on the night stand said **9:48** in the morning.

The reply came back at 10:10: "Good work, Mister Plett. You just made it in time. I had a blanket email with an attachment about to go out to a hundred of your contacts."

No surprise he had Chandler's cell number. **What now, fucker?** Chandler texted.

"Check your door."

Christ, I must have just missed him. Chandler raced to the door. The same brown paper wrapping. His own name in block lettering.

Inside the room, he opened it. A pair of nondescript USB sticks, one holding his ladyboy video; the other was task number three.

A map and a menu. Asterisks marked circled restaurants. The menu consisted of dishes noted in felt-tip black ink below each restaurant. His task was to eat that particular dish at each stop in an orbit around the city involving different prefectures. He had 24 hours to eat eight meals with his GoPro donned to record every bite. The note concluded with a two-word threat: **Or else.**

After his first three stops, Chandler understood the humiliation, not to mention the gastric danger involved, and he knew the blackmail would never end. These weren't five-star dining venues. They were dodgy, unhygienic holes-in-the-wall with no American equivalent. The worst greasy spoon or roadside truck-stop diner could not compare to them. He needed a cast-iron stomach to consume the gelatinous, foul-tasting slop that began with raw chicken breast sashimi followed by natto, a stringy, slimy soybean concoction that tripped his gag reflex after just the first spoonful.

Nauseated and vomiting into the curbs while passersby walked around him like a rock-splitting bow wave, he ingested a grotesque medley of meats, fish, and offal that came from stomachs, intestines, and knee joints with exotic names at every stop on his gustatory pilgrimage from Hell. Everything smelled rancid, some reminded him of dirty athletic socks. Others were so pungent that he had no mental image other than of brackish swamps where disgusting things swam or crawled out of them.

His final dish was basashi served with dollops of putrid soy sauce—raw horse meat—in a dining establishment in a back alley that no health inspector in the States would have approved for one minute. That was a gourmet dish compared to what had already gone down his gullet.

He lay in bed that night with a bloated stomach and rumbling innards, too sick to get to the toilet in time. Bouts of diarrhea and vomiting tossed him on the bed all night long like a shipwrecked sailor. The smell from his room wafted into the hallway and was so offensive that nearby guests complained to management. When they opened the door to his room, the clerk stutter-stepped backward as though a wall of stench fell on him. He was delirious when they called an ambulance. A professional cleaning service that handled crime scenes was called.

Weeks of searching paid off. She liked to shop downtown. Chandler almost didn't recognize her. She still had fine legs and a high can for a short woman, but she was adding pounds thanks to sugar daddy's wallet.

He followed her back to their bungalow a block from the Temple of the Reclining Buddha in the Phra Nakhon District.

Whenever he left the house, Chandler was alert. By then, he had the man's itinerary down pat. It didn't vary. After his morning coffee, the man took a long stroll alone on the beach.

He'd already picked out the spot for the ambush. The closest beachgoers were a hundred yards distant and separated by a small cove that blocked the view and provided privacy.

"Hello, motherfucker. Got any more tasks for me?"

"I beg your pardon, sir," the silver-haired oaf in the Hawaiian shirt responded. "Do I know you?"

"You do. I brought you a gift from Japan," Chandler said, beaming. "I was unable to give it to you there." He brought the cane out from behind his back.

"You have me mistaken for someone else." The man didn't take his eyes off the thick bamboo cane resting against Chandler's thigh.

Chandler didn't have all his physical strength back yet, but he had more than enough for the fat slug in beach shorts with parrots on them, who bolted for his house.

Chandler laughed when the man tumbled, did a face-plant where the waves lapped the shoreline. He got up, sputtering sand, craning his neck to see Chandler approach at an easy pace. Like a crab scuttling sideways, the overweight senior citizen tried to work himself up to stand but managed only to get a few feet on all fours before collapsing back into the sand, blubbering. The waves sloshed around his hands and feet, making the man's next attempt to rise even feebler.

"What?" Chandler gasped in fake surprise. "You don't want your present?"

"Please... Please," the obese man gasped. "It was all a joke for the film. You shouldn't have—"

The first blow took him over the right eyebrow and opened up the flesh in a bright scimitar of a gash. The second was Chandler's golf swing with a 9 iron that cracked the man's jaw and dislocated it so completely that the mandible flapped loose. The next blow to the back of the man's big head was the coup de grâce.

Or else it might have been the blow that took half his IQ points off and would have pleased his docile mistress back in the bungalow. Chandler didn't know and didn't care because he was running all out, the bamboo cane tossed into the ocean before he'd gone ten yards. He sprinted back down the beach, toward the crowd at the shoreline in front of the luxury resort hotels.

Chandler sped by them, his feet wings, his body canted into the offshore breeze. He raced into the wind, shirt flapping, his heart light. His flight out was leaving in an hour. He was already fashioning a new episode for his next vlogging adventure.

Chandler Plett was never going home, never going back to obscurity. He'd conquered fear and found immortality. He knew, as he ran with animal grace, that he was one of the ones favored by the gods.

Author Bio

Twitter: @TomHaftmann   Instagram: @RobbTW1234

Born and raised in Ohio, Robb White has published several noir novels as well as genre and mainstream stories in various magazines and anthologies under such pseudonyms as Robb T. White and Terry White. Nominated for a Derringer Award, his crime story, "Inside Man," was selected for Best American Mystery Stories 2019.

White has two hardboiled private-eye series. His latest is *Fade to Black: Noir Stories of Grifters, Drifters, & Unlovable Losers.*

Zombie Whorehouse

By Sebastian Vice & Paige Johnson

Who's more in need of rebranding than pedophiles? Leave marketing up to me. I'm the lady up for the challenge. Tall tasks come with heftier rewards and I'm looking to pay my rent by tenfold, forever. One day, I'll make Epstein Island look like pussy shit. Make Ghislaine Maxwell look like a haggard hanger-on.

I always tell my clients not to worry, I understand their unfair lot in life, their lecherous leprous reputation. The problem isn't the proclivity, it's the harm to others once things go beyond the mindset—and our business model can mitigate that. After all, what makes a person *really* a person?

Their cognitive ability. Their ability to function. Listen, I know people say children are already lower on that spectrum than adults, but I'm talking about consciousness—not consciences. If someone can't remember, can't fully feel or wrap their heads around what's happening to them—attach to any of the moral fiber of the society they're born into—what's the harm?

Necrophilia is nasty, but who's injured?

Cannibalism is gross but, without a murder, who's hurt?

Our operation functions in a similar fashion. Here at ZW Industries, we grow vegetables, if you catch my drift. Let me walk you around my garden.

I've explained it a million times to prospective investors or clients, showing I commiserate. Everyone has degenerate urges. Women turn rape fantasies into *New York Times* Best Sellers they repaint romantic. Step-parent/sibling porn is more popular than The Beatles. "Daddy" and "Mommy" are replacing "baby" as the Zillenial go-to when it comes to gushing over popstars, actors, or whatever piece of ass they see strolling the streets/tied up in their bedsheets.

Chronically online is the new normal, and dark web whispers seep into the Clearnet zeitgeist. I mean, what teenage dude hasn't heard of that horse-fucking "Mr. Hands" video, or watched The Pain Olympics as a "joke"? And it's become a meme that white girls fuck dogs—there's that Rusty Cage song about it that had six million views before it got taken down by YouTube after they stole the ad revenue. Take a closer look around. Furries and zoophiles saturate Tumblr, Twitter, and TikTok like a cumrag. Our brains marinate in that Freudian id sludge.

Cultural rot. I drink it like raw milk, water my garden with it. Societal crumbling, I crave that slippery slope. It gets me wet, erects my wallet.

Speaking of, let's not get it twisted. Zoey Walsh doesn't cater to brokies, those *Pedo Park* trailer poors with neckbeards and no finesse. No ambition or caution to build their income before partaking in kiddie fiddling. The fucking dolts.

And on the subject of semantics or setting the record straight: The public classifies all underage sexual relations as pedophilia. However, a commitment to facts reveals someone is only a pedophile if their primary attraction is children under the age of 13 and the philiac only has to be 16+. So if a 30-year-old fucks a 15-year-old, he's not a pedophile. If you hate these distinctions, take it up with the DSM-5.

People bitch that ephebophilia is nit-picking but I ask, is quadruple homicide worse than mono-murder or not? Right. Anyway, it's essential to recognize there's no known cure for pedophilia or the like. You can't therapy your way to victory.

Women like me grew up on diets of D.A.R.E and This-Is-Your-Brain-On-Drugs commercials. Blanket statements and bullshit. What held promise was AI-generated child porn. I heard a lecture where a man discredited such advances as encouraging perversion. However, isn't it better for pedophiles to blast their loads in privacy, and not in some young lad's asshole?

These observations are paramount in developing what my perverted patrons affectionately dub Zombie Whorehouse.

We have several rules for admissions. First, no criminal record. Second, no filming. Third, a written and video confession admitting to their proclivities (if they squeal, we reveal). Fourth, don't damage the property. Abide by the rules, don't act a fool, and you can use your tool. (We're all about fun taglines.)

We even offer membership packages (punch cards pending).

Tier 1 ($xx,ooo Yearly): buffet-style all-you-can-fuck (limit one hour a day)

Tier 2 ($xx,ooo Yearly): Once-a-week fuck (limit one hour a week)

Tier 3 ($xx,ooo Yearly): Once-a-month fuck (limit one hour a month)

Specials:

Platinum ($1M): rent the whorehouse for a month

Gold ($500K): rent the whorehouse for two weeks

Silver ($250k): rent the whorehouse for a week

Bronze ($75K): weekend special

We are a small operation. Never use real names so, if one gets pinched, the rest don't. And in this business, only a virgin trusts anyone.

I'm Miss Black (Co-Owner)

There's The Accountant (Co-Owner)

There's The Detective

There's The Physician

There's The Fixer Boys (Mr. X & Mr. Z)

You obviously won't find us on a map. And you won't know what we front as our business. Maybe I own a bar. Perhaps I own a laundromat. Maybe go fuck yourself.

The Fixer Boys drive me to a local skyline cafe. The Detective procured a prospective client. We don't meet with clients unless they make a $10K down payment and submit the relevant incriminating evidence.

The Fixer Boys hang out in the parking lot.

I approach his sleek silver high-top overlooking the city. A Jameson, neat, sits before him half-drained. "Jack, I presume?"

He nods and gestures for me to sit.

"This is an interview process," I make clear as I smooth my skirt suit and sit down.

The waitress fills me a glass of water with whole circles of cucumber and lemon. They bob like the fresh veggies that come into ZW for a hosing—first-housing and de-lousing.

When she departs, I notice several empty tables between us. Think this man could be a cop. Wouldn't be the first time. The Detective is usually good at spotting 'em, but nobody's perfect. "The files you sent were suggestive," I say with my typical playful brow-raise.

He looks around the panorama of sunset and steel skyscrapers, leans in. "I know the rules."

I nod. "Yeah? And cops can snort blow. Cops can kill niggers. Cops can lie." I wink. "But all the best cops die." I let the room breathe. "We need an additional file... Just to be sure we don't need to make you bacon."

Sweat pours from his brow. I can almost hear it sizzle. "Okay..."

"A test," I say. "Relax. If you pass, and have the cash, we got your disease."

The Accountant calls our initiation ritual The Kiddie Fucker Haze. Possession of child pornography can land you in prison for an average of 70 months (a little under six years). With VPNs, the dark web, and the overall low-IQ of police, politicians, and juries, conviction rates are low. We can fix the courts. We can ensue a squealer doesn't last a week.

But that takes time and money. We value both.

We need a prospective client caught in the act to file away as blackmail. And if Jack doesn't comply, we double tap him, float his ass down the Mississippi, and The Detective frames it as a suicide. Sounds crazy or Clinton-esque, but he got a motorcycle accident ruled as a suicide by gunshot—without holes in the helmet.

You can sell the average retard anything if it comes from a man in a suit. Just look who we elect.

"These are real kids?" the man specifies through his hood. "Not replicas like advanced Real Dolls or some shit?"

The Physician sits in the passenger seat, doing lines of coke. "They're biological."

"Is making me wear this hood really necessary?"

"Save the questions for the warehouse."

The Detective follows behind us, keeping distance. The Fixer Boys remain silent, an unusual feat. On these trips, they usually argue over whether *Star Wars* or *Star Trek* is better, which spinoff is superior.

We round a corner onto a red dirt road.

Few more miles and we unhood our man.

"A forest," he says.

"We got ourselves a fuckin' Rhodes Scholar here," The Physician hoots.

"We'll be outside," The Fixer Boys say in unison.

The Detective pulls up beside us.

"Let's go inside," I say. "You'll like what we—"

"Fresh blood, eh?" Gary, a long-time patron, asks of Jack while exiting the building. "Buddy, once you get a taste of the goods..." He makes a wolfish howl. "You'll never want to leave."

"That good?" Jack asks.

"Fuckin' A!" Gary says, uncrinkling his tie.

"Keep it movin', Mr. Hart," I say.

When we enter the waiting room, Miss Star is dancing to Belinda Carlisle's "Heaven is a Place on Earth."

"Is she—" Jack starts.

"Yes, darling. Of course. I like 'em young." She winks. "You boys don't get to have all the fun." She blows him a kiss and goes back to bopping.

I insist he sit. "We need to set up. Give us 10-15 minutes."

The warehouse proper often smells of sex, the kind of stench that clings to your clothes long after you leave, as if the air has hands clutching your throat.

"You fail any of this," The Detective says, snapping his notebook shut, "well, I don't think I need to tell you the consequences."

Jack looks at me, eyes pleading. "And if I do it? Then what?"

"Then you're in," I say.

He nods, his hands finally steadying as he picks up the camcorder. "Okay."

We leave him to it, watching through a one-way mirror.

He fumbles with the camcorder, face drained of blood. Guess he doesn't like voyeurs.

"You think he'll crack?" Mr. X asks, lighting a cigarette.

"Shall we bet?" The Detective asks.

"Fuckin' Hell," Mr. Z says. "He better not. My back hurts too much to dig another ditch."

"Ten large he doesn't crack," Mr. X bets.

The Detective smirks. "I'll take that deal."

Jack takes longer than most, but doesn't crack. For all his reluctance, he does a fine job.

"Goddamn it!" The Detective curses.

"Cough it up, bitch."

The Detective throws an envelope at Mr. X.

As per the deal, Jack goes on to confess to the camera like a reality show schlub. The words pour out of him like vomit, staining the air with every sick thought he's ever had. He plugs in the USB, fingers trembling, and uploads the horrors to our servers.

When we come back in, he's shaking, clutching the camcorder like a lifeline.

"Well done," I say, slapping him on the back. I replace the electronics with a menu of our services. "Welcome to the family."

The Fixer Boys escort him out, but The Detective stays behind, flipping through his notebook again.

"Think he'll last?" I ask.

The Detective shrugs, cutting a line of white on his compact mirror. "I don't care. I'm not the hole-digger."

I remember my childhood house—the cracked linoleum in the kitchen, the stench of mildew from the bathroom, the sound of his boots dragging across the floor after another long night at the bar. My father, a towering figure—not in stature, but in presence—shrank a room when he entered.

He wasn't always a monster. Or maybe he was, and I was too young to notice. I used to wait by the window, tiny hands pressed against the glass, watching for his truck to pull into the driveway.

He'd stumble in, reeking of whiskey, and lift me into the air, calling me his princess.

But somewhere between the laughing nights and the yelling ones, I stopped being his princess.

By the time I was ten, he introduced me to weaponized love. My mother bore the brunt of it, and I— Well, I learned to disappear. Learned to shrink into corners and swallow my screams when the shouting turned to fists. But even shadows can't hide forever.

One night, he found me.

It was quick. Brutal. The kind of thing that stains you, that turns your body into a prison, and fragments your psyche. The kind of torment that leaves you with glass eyes.

He left me on the floor, tangled in my *VeggieTales* sheets, crumpled like a discarded doll, and I remember thinking—not crying, just thinking—that I wasn't scared of him anymore. The worst had happened and I hated him more than I feared him.

The next morning, I packed a bag and left.

Just like that. No goodbye, no note. I walked to the bus station, sat on the hard, cold bench and waited for the first ride out of town. I didn't care where it was going.

Life on the streets isn't kind to anyone but I'd already learned how to be invisible. Stealing came naturally. So did lying. People see a scared, dirty kid and either pity you or ignore you. I used both to my advantage.

Survival is a kind of artistry, you know.

By 16, I wasn't just surviving—I was thriving. I met a man named Marcus. A charmer, slick as oil, with a smile that could sell you your own death. He said he saw potential in me, though I knew what he really saw: discolored clay easy to mold. He taught me how to con, how to kill without leaving a trace, how to look someone in the eye and make them believe you're their salvation while you're picking their pocket.

"People are tools," he used to say. "Use them or they'll use you."

I believed him but, in my naivety, didn't think he'd use me.

Marcus liked power. Liked control. And he liked to remind me that I had none.

One day, he went too far. Underestimated me, as men like him always do. I waited until he was drunk, until his guard was down, and then I slit his throat.

No hesitation. No second thoughts. I watched the light flicker from his eyes.

I felt nothing.

From there, it was like a door had opened. A new world. A world where I wasn't the victim anymore. I became Miss Black— a ghost, a myth, a whisper in the dark.

I learned to navigate the cracks in the system, to exploit the rot at its core. People like to pretend they're good, but, strip away the lies, and we're all just animals.

Am I a villain?

Maybe.

Maybe not.

Does it matter? Heroes and villains all wind up in holes.

So, in the end, who gives a fuck?

The system chews people up and spits them out, and I've simply learned to bite back. Survival isn't pretty. It's not noble. But it's all I've ever known.

I'm not some sob story.

I'm not a broken little girl looking for redemption.

I'm just a woman who stopped being afraid.

Our day starts before sunrise, the air in the basement thick with industrial chemicals. Most clients don't notice or, if they do, they know better than to complain. What matters is the upkeep. A fresh coat of foundation here, a clean skirt, and a hygiene ritual.

Can't have the merchandise looking too close to death, even if the clients don't seem to mind.

"I checked our stock," I tell The Physician. "We need more cocaine and Viagra."

"I don't get these people."

"Coke keeps 'em going—"

"—And the Viagra keeps 'em hard."

"Exactly," I say. "Who wants to fuck with a half-hard dick?"

"And who cares about heart attacks when your dick is wet?" The Physician shakes his head, knowing better than anyone people like to double up or triple their vices.

I slide on gloves and lean over one of our veggies—Delilah, the name we assigned after her first week. Her lips are cracked, skin a patchwork of decay and quick fixes. Last night, a client got rough. Tore at her cheek until it hung loose, flapping like wet paper.

I sew it back into place, my needle slipping through dead flesh with practiced ease. "She'll heal, right?"

The Physician nods.

"The Fixer Boys work him over?"

"Not too bad. He drops over a million into this place a year."

"Good as new, Delilah," I say, stepping back to admire my handiwork. Her eyes—cloudy, lifeless—stare past me.

The truth is, they all look the same after a while. They're just bodies. Inventory.

Upstairs, the front door unbolts after the bell sounds and guards enter the passkey. A morning customer is here. "Welcome back," I say bloodlessly over the intercom. "You know the drill—pick your poison, pay up front."

The man nods, not even glancing toward the security camera as he walks past. That's the thing about this place—no one speaks, no one asks questions. Not about how we keep them moving, not about the logistics of life support, not about what happens when the veggies can't be patched up anymore.

They just want what they paid for. Say what you will about Capitalism: You get what you pay for.

The rooms fill up quickly. There's a line, as there always is on Fridays. A businessman in a rumpled suit leans against the wall, scrolling through his phone. A trust-fund college kid taps his foot, eyes darting towards the door every few seconds like he's afraid someone might see him. They're all the same: desperate, hollow men with just enough cash to indulge their most base desires.

The Physician calls it a well-oiled machine. I call it something else entirely, though I stopped trying to label it a long time ago.

In the back room, one of the newer girls, Ruby, makes a wet, guttural sound. She's glitching again—spasming in that jerky, unnatural way that happens when the thrusting gets too vigorous.

I grab the cattle prod from the corner and jab it into the client's ribs.

He collapses to the floor. "Fucking bitch!"

"This is your second warning," I say like a kindergarten teacher. "A third winds you up in a hole."

By noon, the place reeks of sweat and something worse. The men file out one by one, some avoiding eye contact, others strutting like they've just conquered the world.

One of them—a middle-aged guy with greasy hair and a nervous tic—pauses at the counter. "She, uh, she remembered me," he says, his voice a mix of pride and unease. "That's... That's normal, right?"

I don't bother answering. I just smile, tight-lipped, and take his money.

In the evening, we clean up. It's the worst part of the job, scrubbing the blood and filth from the rooms, repairing the veggies for another night.

As I mop the floor, The Physician leans against the doorway, lighting a cigarette. "Good day, huh?"

I glance at the pile of fat stacks, then at the rows of empty, staring eyes in the holding room. "Yeah," I say. "Another day in paradise."

And tomorrow, it'll start all over again.

"Something bothers me."

The Physician cocks his head.

"A client said a girl remembers him."

"Impossible. I take great care to ensure all of them are pronounced brain dead."

"You sure?"

The Physician scowls. "Who's more reliable: me or one of the jerkoff fuckin' clients?"

We check the girl and she's unresponsive.

"See?" he says, shaking his head. "Fucko was probably just tryin' to brag. Or one of those nouveau riche trying to get a discount."

I nod.

The Accountant meets with me. In all our years doing business, I've only seen him half a dozen times. Today, he makes an appearance at the warehouse. He's never come here.

Whatever his façade job is, it must demand only the finest attire. "This suit costs more than most make in a year," he boasts outside, lighting up a cigar. A cool breeze whips the smoke around. "I detest coming here. But I have bad news."

"Well," I say, "don't keep me in suspense."

"Several of our front businesses went under."

"Fuck." Not more.

"Our nice little fast-food chain is done."

"That leaves..." I scratch my head. "Just..."

"The bookstore, and music store." He pauses. "Even diehards don't buy enough CDs or vinyl anymore. I give it a few months."

"So how—"

"—Not to worry, darling." He puffs the cigar. "I invested in a few coffee shops, and—" He pauses, grinning. "A medical supply company. How's that for irony?"

"So, what's the bad news? The truly bad news?"

"Hope you and the crew have savings..."

I hold my breath.

"We're broke now. Better start living a more Spartan lifestyle for the foreseeable future."

I hold the breath even while rounding up the crew to explain the situation. Of course they aren't pleased—goddamn retards haven't saved a dime.

But I have.

"I'll need money for bribes," The Detective insists.

I nod. "I'll cover it. We'll be alright."

The Physician scrutinizes me with eyes of liquid nitrogen. "I hope so."

The day after I downgrade my penthouse to a discreet walk-up, I sit outside the warehouse, smoking what The Physician calls Snoop-Strength-Weed. It begins snowing, and a few customers trickle in. December is usually a slow month for some reason. Perhaps Ebenezer's ghosts visit them.

"Damn good operation," Jack says upon exiting the building. "Well worth the hazing and price of admission."

I nod. "Yeah."

"The strangest fuckin' thing though..." He pauses. "One of the girls...talked."

I sober up like someone's slammed my head into ice water. "What?"

"I thought they were brain dead?"

"They are."

"Can brain dead girls—"

"—They are!" I take a final toke, and fling the joint into snow. "Safe trip home, Jack!"

He nods.

The grotesque parody of life we induce is like acid on the soul. For years, you tell yourself it's just business, you contort your rationalizations to say what's broken is beyond fixing. No one mourns the fallen when the whole world's a graveyard.

One of the girls talked.

I can't shake Jack's statement. It haunts me like Poe's "Tell-Tale Heart."

She isn't the prettiest one in the lineup. Her jaw hangs a little too loose, the stitching around her neck rushed and jagged. Marcus calls her Amber—a recycled name for a new product, just another body with a story no one cares to hear.

It starts small. A flicker in her eyes when I pass her holding room. Not the milky vacancy I'm used to. This is different—sharp, deliberate, as though seeing me for the first time.

I tell myself it's nothing. Random muscle twitches, lingering neural signals.

That's what The Physician always says when I bring up anything out of the ordinary. "Meat doesn't think," he says with a shrug, chewing the end of his cigar.

Something tells me Amber isn't a mere meat puppet.

The first time she moves, really moves, I gasp as if a knife's sliding into my lungs. I was cleaning up after one of the regulars—a man I can't stand to look at for too long without wanting to shove his face through a window.

Amber is sprawled on the bed, her arms limp and askew like a broken doll. Her client had been rough; one of her fingers bends at an unnatural angle, and there's a sickening crack in her forearm where the bone split beneath the skin.

I'm about to call The Fixer Boys to work the client over when she turns her head.

Her eyes lock onto mine.

Not a glance, not a fluke. Her head moves slowly, deliberately, and her lips part just enough to let out the faintest hoarse whisper: "Help me."

I freeze. The room goes quiet except for our heartbeats.

She shouldn't be able to say anything—whatever spark of humanity is supposed to be dead. That's what makes this operation work. That's what makes it "ethical."

But Amber spoke.

I don't tell anyone. I think maybe I imagined it, that the job has finally gotten under my skin. But the next time I see her, she moves again. A slight twitch of her fingers when I enter the room. Her head tilted ever so slightly toward me, like she's waiting for me to notice.

And I do.

I start watching her. Noticing the tiny things: the way her eyes follow me when no one else is looking, the barely perceptible tremor in her hands when The Physician comes too close.

I swear she clenches her fist when one of the clients touches her face.

They don't notice. No one ever notices.

Except me.

One night, when The Detective and Physician are in the back counting the day's take, I go to her room. I tell myself it's to check on her, to fix the torn stitching in her arm, but deep down I know it's something else. I need to know.

"Amber," I say quietly, kneeling by her side.

Her head turns toward me again, slower this time, like it takes effort.

Her lips move. No sound comes out, but the word is unmistakable: "Please."

My stomach churns. I want to ask her what she means, but I can't form the words. Instead, I reach for her hand, the one with the crooked finger and, for a moment, I think she'll grab mine.

She doesn't. But her eyes—God, her eyes—burn into me with something that feels too alive, too human to ignore.

It isn't until later at night, alone in the staff quarters, that I remember her file. Every veg has one. A name, an age, a cause of brain death. Most of them come in as Jane or John Does, the dregs of a world that forgot them long before they arrived here. Amber's file is no different. But as I read through it, something gnaws at me.

She'd been local. The daughter of a waitress at the sky lounge down the street. Her mother is 24 years old. Her photo stares back at me, grainy but unmistakable—the same sharp eyes, the same pale face. But it isn't her death certificate that stops me.

It's the police report attached.

Her cause of death wasn't an accident. It wasn't an overdose. It was attempted murder. And she obviously wasn't brain dead.

She'd been "killed" by The Physician, the crime covered up by The Detective.

I pour a strong drink and listen to the two of them joke while counting the money. My mind turns to white noise. My body goes numb.

The next time I see her, she doesn't wait for me to speak. Her lips move, her voice barely a whisper, but the words cut through me like a winter wind.

"They all remember."

I stumble back, nearly tripping over the corner of the bed. She doesn't move after that. Her head lolls to the side, her body slack and lifeless once more.

"They all remember," I repeat.

Every touch. Every word. Every moment of violence.

I walk into the woods, and sit on a tree stump.

I remove a pistol, and place it against my temple.

"Fuck this."

AuthOr BiO

Site: Outcast-Press.com   Instagram: @OutcastPress

Sebastian Vice is founder of Outcast Press (publisher of this very anthology). His fiction has been nominated for Best Of The Net since 2021 and he authored the poetry book *Homo Mortalis: Meditations on Memento Mori*. You can find his feeder fetish story in the *HUNGER* anthology (Urban Pigs Press), analingus story in *Anxious Nothings*, and a heartfelt epistolary about homosexuality in *Mirrors Reflecting Shadows*.

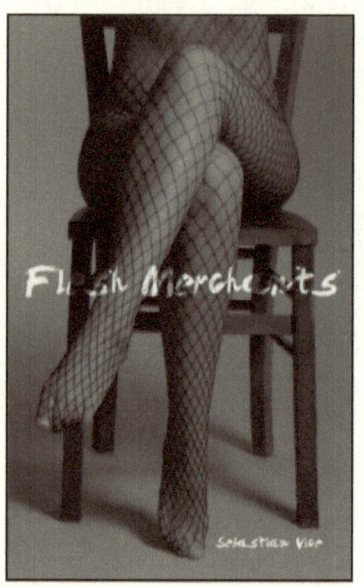

Vice has many projects forthcoming, including the story collection *Flesh Merchants*, the '70s abortion noir *Driver* and philosophical apocalyptic novella, *Only The Numb Remain. Flesh Merchants II* is slated to collaborate with Paige Johnson surrounding themes of sex and death.

The Name Of Your First pet

By Tom Leins

The sodium lights outside the Sunshine Café give the worn Formica furnishings a spectral appearance. The café is mercifully empty, and I can count the other customers on the bruised knuckles of one hand.

The woman is middle-aged. Elegantly dressed, but disturbingly ugly. She's wearing a fawn-coloured trouser-suit and too much gold jewellery.

"Mr. Rey?"

I nod.

"Fluffy Carmichael."

"Seriously?" I ask.

She rolls her thickly lashed eyes. "You may be too young to remember, but I originated the trend of combining the name of my first pet with my mother's maiden name—in the Westcountry, at least. It was celebrated at the time, but the very concept has been turned into a damned schoolboy joke." She sits down and lights a cigarette but stubs it out immediately. "I've been informed that you specialise in finding missing persons?"

I nod.

"I'd like you to locate an ex-colleague of mine."

"Ex-colleague? As in...?"

She removes a creased VHS cover from her handbag and slides it across the table. *Spunk Drunk 2: Tartt with a Heart.*

The hot-pink block letters on the artwork identify the leading lady as Treacle Tartt. She's wearing nylon gloves, plastic jewellery, and nothing else.

Her sly smile reminds me of my ex-wife, Alouette. The night Alouette and I met, we had sex in her late father's bed. The musty, creaky deathbed of a big man that sagged badly in the middle. Looking back, it's hard to think of a less erotic scenario.

"How long has she been missing?" I ask.

Fluffy Carmichael lights another cigarette and lets it smoulder between her knuckles this time. "Three weeks."

"Have you checked hospitals, psych-wards, morgues...?"

Fluffy snorts. "Psych-wards? Treacle is no more unhinged than you, I, or that man over there." With her cigarette, she gestures to the counterman, as he runs a grotty rag across the nearest table, leaving a thick, brown smear in his wake.

Fluffy grimaces.

"Do you have a more recent photograph?" I ask.

She shakes her head.

"What about a real name?"

"If I knew it, I'd surely tell you."

Fluffy's large breasts are accentuated by her open-necked blouse. From across the table, I can smell this afternoon's sun oil on her body.

She leans towards me and lowers her voice. "Back in my day, if you wanted to earn a living, you had to pull up your knickers and get on with it, Mr. Rey."

I stare at her, uncomprehending. *Pull up your knickers?*

She prods a bright pink nail at me. "Will you take the case or not, Rey? You're the first man on my list, but not the last."

I stare at the VHS cover. "Pinky Sharp," I blurt.

"Excuse me?"

"Sure. I'll take the job, Ms. Carmichael."

She looks confused at my random outburst but removes a wad of banknotes from her purse regardless. "£500 now. Another £500 when you find her. I trust that will prove sufficient?"

"*If* I find her. Not *when* I find her."

She grunts, already halfway to the door. She's about to say something but thinks better of it and steps out into the dank, early evening air.

I unscrew the top of my hip-flask and splash another shot into my tepid coffee, before swallowing the whole lot down with a grimace.

Pinky was a rescue shelter cat. My first—and only—pet. In February 1984, he was wrapped in a bin-bag with a breezeblock and drowned in our shallow, scummy garden pond by my mother's shallow, scummy boyfriend, Leon. That was shortly before the pair of them abandoned my half-sister and me next to a dual carriageway—never to be seen again.

I carefully fold the VHS cover, neatly bisecting Treacle Tartt's naked torso, and slip it into my jacket pocket.

It's fair to say that missing women are something of a preoccupation.

Two hours later.

Church Street, Paignton.

In this town, too many people linger in the dark—out of sight, out of mind.

I stare at the creased *Spunk Drunk 2* VHS cover.

The reverse of the sleeve is largely illegible: smudged and crinkled from various spillages and bodily fluids. As a result, I can only make out one name on the credits, that of the lighting technician: Benjamin Brinham.

Benny Brinham worked as a light tech for the BBC down in Plymouth, and his sporadic dalliances with adult material were just a way of earning extra beer money on the weekends. His inglorious career hit the skids when he was arrested after drugging and sodomising a 59-year-old department store employee called Barbara Browne. It was in the Mayflower Street

West carpark in the late '90s. Barbara turned out to be the fourth woman who Benny had attacked in that same crumbling carpark.

He was sentenced to 30 years in HMP Dartmoor, only to be let out last year due to ill health.

I ring Benny's doorbell, more out of hope than expectation.

I have a knuckle-duster in my jacket pocket and a pig-knife in my boot. As the door starts to creak open, I slip my fingers into the brass knuckles, ready to inflict instant pain on the rotten old fucker. A lot of people pour scorn on the *punch first/ask questions later* technique, but I have always found it to be a brutally effective way of doing business.

The girl who answers the door looks more surprised than I do.

I relax my grip and wipe my sweaty hand on my jeans.

"What the fuck do you want?" she asks amiably.

She has red hair, tied back, and a thick covering of freckles. She's wearing a purple velour tracksuit and I notice she has a high-tar cigarette tucked behind each ear.

"I need to see Benny. Is he around?"

She cackles nastily. "Well, he's not fucking going anywhere, is he? Come on, follow me."

I traipse down the hallway after her, into the lounge, and come face-to-face with Benny Brinham's pale, desiccated body. The room smells of shit, piss, and bleach—in that order. Thin, plastic tubes snake into his nose, his mouth, his cock.

The girl lights one cigarette and offers me the other.

I shake my head and she tucks it back behind her ear.

"My name's Yvonne. I'm his carer," she offers.

"Joe," I grunt, unwilling to provide any further information about myself.

She puffs on the ciggie and stares at the cloud of smoke as it lingers above Benny's withered body. She glances at me curiously. "I've been with him for nearly two years, and you're the first person who has ever come to visit."

I shrug.

"I'm not surprised. He wasn't exactly a charmer..." She exhales another mouthful of smoke. "Benny was a criminal, right?"

"He was a sex offender," I clarify.

I'm sure I would be a criminal in most people's eyes, and I feel the need to draw a distinction between me and a shitbag like Brinham.

She smirks at me. "They say that, in Paignton, you're never more than ten feet away from a registered sex offender. Maybe I need to start carrying a tape measure."

I return the smirk. "Maybe you should. May I?"

She steps away and I edge closer to Benny's prone form.

His translucent flesh is stretched taut, revealing far too much of the skull beneath the skin. He's in his 60s but looks at least 30 years older.

"What's he dying of?" I ask her over my shoulder.

"How long have you got?" She sighs.

I lean over him, seeing if I can detect any recognition in his yellow eyes.

"Kill...me..." he mutters over the ragged whine of his breathing apparatus.

I shake my head.

This is how monsters check out. Wasting away in sheltered accommodation, under the watchful eye of a worker paid minimum wage to wipe their arse and mop up their dehydrated piss.

I walk over to the cheap pine bookshelf next to the back wall. There are no books on it, only videotapes. Hundreds of fucking videotapes. On the floor, next to the shelving unit are a boxy, unplugged TV and a dusty, ancient-looking VCR. "Does he ever ask to watch any of these videos?" I ask Yvonne.

"If he did, I'd have to unplug his fucking breathing apparatus," she chuckles. "Not enough plug sockets, what with all of the shit he's hooked up to."

I run my finger along the greasy plastic spines until I find the one I'm looking for. Benny clearly had a well-ordered mind, as the videos have been filed in alphabetical order. My mind is about as well-ordered as a burning bin-bag.

Spunk Drunk 2: Tartt with a Heart has been placed between the original *Spunk Drunk* and *Spunk Drunk 3: Gobbles Guzzles Globules*. I remove the latter out of curiosity.

Gobbles Gorman has a bottle-blonde dye-job and a lazy eye. Her wonky smile unnerves me, so I replace the video and remove *Spunk Drunk 2*. I scrutinise the credits for a name I recognise and quickly hit paydirt. "Mind if I borrow this?" I ask.

Yvonne shrugs and makes a lazy 'wanker' gesture at me. "Whatever floats your boat, boss."

I peel a bill off the wad that Fluffy Carmichael gave me and hand it to her. "Buy yourself a drink when you knock off."

She looks disbelievingly at the £50 note. "Is this real?"

Realer than Gobbles Gorman's tits, I think.

I flash her a small, grim smile and see myself out.

The Dirty Lemon public house, Dartmouth Road.

Larry Tinto is a dead-eyed day-drinker whose conversation is weaker than his pulse. He is also, it turns out, my friendly neighbourhood pornographer. I always assumed he was a boozy fantasist, the kind of guy whose cinematic career began with a borrowed camcorder and ended with a mattress in the back of a Transit Van. That was until I noticed his name on the VHS cover for *Spunk Drunk* 2.

Director of Photography.

The film was produced by Caruso Industries, back in the glory days. Better known as the Fuck Factory, Caruso's tawdry empire operated out of a warehouse on an abandoned trading estate outside Plymouth. He flooded the Westcountry with cheap, locally produced skin-flicks for almost a decade.

When Caruso died, the helm was taken over by his right-hand man, Teddy Shingles, a disgraced gynaecologist and one-time mob doctor who earned his stripes treating the Andretti Family's working girls for STDs and minor lacerations.

The Teddy Shingles era played out like a poor-quality facsimile. A lukewarm, reheated cover of a previously enjoyable product. After ten months with Teddy's unsteady, liver-spotted hand on the tiller, the Fuck Factory was a bleary-eyed husk of a business: creatively and financially bankrupt. The factory doors were padlocked shut and what was left of the talent pool scurried to Devon's deepest, darkest corners like stomped rats.

I clear my throat.

Up close, everything about Larry Tinto looks yellowed, decayed, nicotine-stained.

"Mind if I have a word, Larry?" I ask.

He hands his cadaverous female companion a crumpled £10 note and asks her to freshen their drinks. She's wearing a fake fur coat and orthopaedic shoes. As she hobbles past me, she looks ravaged and could be any age between 40 and 70.

"What d'you think of Porky Perkins?" he asks.

"That's Porky Perkins?!"

He leers at me. "She's still got it, Rey!"

"Whatever 'it' is, it looks terminal, mate."

He glares at me. "What can I do you for?"

I pass him the VHS cover. "You know her?"

"Treacle? How could I fucking forget her! Wooden delivery, sounded like she was in a ruddy hostage video—but that girl could give a corpse a hard-on."

"Any idea where she might be?"

He sighs, sadly. "No idea, son. Not seen her for donkey's years." He looks up at me, twitching like he's got a bad case of pubic lice.

I pat him on the shoulder, and he flinches. "I'll see you around, Larry."

"I fucking hope not, Rey," he mutters.

I order another pint of Kronenbourg and take a seat next to the cigarette machine, keeping my eyes fixed on Larry Tinto.

He starts prodding at an old Nokia with his spindly fingers. Across the table, Porky Perkins sips her glass of Blue Nun in silence.

I drain my pint and walk across to them.

"Still here, Rey?" he grumbles.

"Looks like it, Larry. Who are you texting, mate?"

He shrugs. "Just a pal. You're never alone with a portable phone."

I remove the handset from his clammy hand and glance down at the block capitals ID on the small screen.

PETER PATTON.

Then I drop the Nokia in his half-drunk pint and bounce his skull off the edge of the table.

Peter Patton's yard is strewn with automotive detritus and rusted tools. I pick my way through the busted engine blocks and dented car parts towards the ramshackle single-story structure at the back of his property. A feint, queasy glow is visible under the ill-fitting steel door.

I retrieve a bent-looking screwdriver from the hard-packed dirt and turn it over in my hand. In my line of work, screwdrivers are useful for popping locks, or popping eyeballs. I lean against the corrugated iron and pop the lock to Patton's workshop, before melting into the gloom. Inside, the first thing that hits me is the weird smell: an eye-watering mixture of piss and bleach.

Patton is an unrepentant bottom-feeder who earned his money buying up patches of wasteland all over Paignton and clamping cars that were parked on his weed-choked territory. People say that he bankrolled the scam using the compensation he got after a surgeon left a needle in him from a minor operation, but I've heard the same story about at least three other local men.

"Who the fuck are you?" he grunts. Patton is a sandy-haired middle-aged man with a beer gut, a switchblade, and a pleather jacket. He has a face like spoiled meat and exudes a lazy sort of malevolence.

I ignore his question, glancing around the room instead.

"This is my place of business!" he protests.

Sure enough, the concrete floor is scattered with rusted wheel-clamps. Along the right-hand wall, he affixed seven rudimentary chipboard shelves, each one sagging with the weight of videotapes balanced on them. On an old TV in the corner, a grainy Turkish grope movie unfurls.

Patton's eyes twinkle. "You're here about the girls, aren't you?" he sneers.

Wait: Girls?

"Who sent you? Bubby Frengers?" he continues. "No, I bet it was Cuddles Calhoun? That loose-lipped bitch needs a ruddy slap!" He looks at me expectantly. His sick eyes shine with glee.

"Fluffy Carmichael," I tell him.

"Ah, Fluffy." He sighs. "I had my first ever wank over her," he mutters wistfully. "She'd be quite the addition to my collection."

I frown. *What collection?*

Then I notice the row of cages against the back wall, behind Patton. I squint through the murk.

A skinny, veiny hand with broken acrylic nails curls around the first set of bars.

"Help...me," the husky voice croaks.

I glance at the laminate cable-tied to the cage. **RANDY CUMMINGS**, it reads.

Randy Cummings crawls into view.

I edge closer, ignoring Patton and his switchblade. I get close enough to see her bloodshot eyes, unruly gray-blonde hair and the stray pubic hair pressed against her thickly applied lip-gloss.

Patton weakly slashes at me with the knife, but I ignore him. He's not a blade-merchant. Far from it. I've only ever seen him cut one man, and that was in the Dirty Lemon, during the transvestite floorshow. If I remember correctly, Patton barely even drew blood that day. I've seen bloodier wank-based injuries in that place.

There's a creaking noise in the next cage as the woman labelled **SPUNKY WILSON** wakes up with a nightmarish screech.

I turn to face Patton, noticing the steel ring of keys clipped to his belt loop. "Are they...dog cages?"

He nods, polishing the blade of his knife on the thigh of his stonewashed jeans, seemingly reluctant to try and stab me a second time. "It's amazing what you can buy online these days. It's even more amazing *who* you can find."

"What you're doing is mental, Patton! You know that, mate?"

He sparks up a Tesco cigarette and exhales a mouthful of smoke in my direction. His glare is hostile, bordering on venomous. "Only dead fish follow the stream, son."

I point towards the third cage in the row, where a skinny, mottled woman with dyed hair and a palsied tremble kneels in silence. "She has to be at least 70! Fucking let her out!"

Patton bares his teeth in a sinister approximation of a smile. "Show some fucking respect! That woman is Gobbles Gorman! She's safe here. She's among friends." He grips the switchblade in front of his belly—nice and tight, like he's holding a stray cock.

Through the broken door of the lock-up, the wind moans like a junkie.

I grab the nearest wheel-clamp and swing the steel in an upwards arc into Patton's jaw, and almost dislocate my right shoulder in the process.

His teeth crunch together with a nasty *crack*.

The clamp clatters to the ground as Patton's knees buckle and he hits the deck.

I step over him and walk across to the final cage. Unlike the others, Patton has draped a paint-splattered dustsheet over it.

I whip the sheet away with an amateur magician's flourish.

Inside, Treacle Tartt's twisted mouth pouts up at me from the rancid mattress. She's still wearing the same nylon gloves and plastic jewellery as she was on the video sleeve.

Nothing else.

Patton crawls towards me, eyes milky, mouth oozing blood. His switchblade scrapes against the concrete as he heaves his lumpen form towards me.

He tries to say something, but all that comes out are blackened chunks of teeth and blacker streaks of viscera.

I tread on his hand, grinding his knuckles into the concrete and forcing him to release the knife with a grunt.

"Pinky Sharp says hello."

Patton's milky eyes swirl as he tries to focus on me.

Then I stomp him so hard, I leave a boot-print on the side of his face.

AuthOr BiO

Twitter: @Tom_Leins

Tom Leins is a crime writer from Paignton, UK. Since 2003, hundreds of his short stories have been published in anthologies, literary journals, and online. His books include *Meat Bubbles & Other Stories, Boneyard Dogs, Ten Pints of Blood, Repetition Kills You, Sharp Knives & Loud Guns*, and *The Good Book: Fairy Tales for Hard Men.*

Leins is also a contributor to *Punk Noir Magazine*, as run by Outcast Press authors Stephen J. Golds and BF Jones. His story, "The First Five People You Meet in Hell," is what got him invited to this anthology. Keep up with him at ThingsToDoInDevonWhenYoureDead.WordPress.com/

More From Our Authors

Horror Sleaze Trash is a long-running website and handcrafted print zine all about the candid and crass. Known for their modern pin-up covers and confessional poetry, *HST* produces daily content and quarterly print issues, as well as larger novella-size poetry volumes.

Headed by Arthur Graham, author of *Piss On It: New and Selected Poems,* as well as *Tall Tales with Short Cocks,* he has featured many Outcast Press authors and readers like Kristin Garth, Paige Johnson, and M P Powers. Look for them and their titillating to tense short stories at www.HorrorSleazeTrash.com

Smalltown Boy

By LG Thomson

Friday night, Soho, late May 1989, and the air is thick with heat leaching from sun-soaked pavements. It's thicker still in the piano bar beside the strip club that's famous enough for sightseers to visit. The bar plays host to tourists of a different ilk. Day-trippers rather than holiday-makers. Night-trippers if you prefer, like vampires, who only come out to play when the sun has set.

The piano bar, like all serious dens of iniquity, is low-lit. Where darkness flourishes, glamour thrives. Faces are sculpted by shadows in this chiaroscuro world. Glittered cheekbones sparkle beneath eyes fringed with lashes thick and false. Glossed lips glisten as they blow streams of smoke Heavenwards. Deadpan drag queens in shimmering gowns pout and pose, their performances punctuated by acidic put-downs and throaty laughter.

Smalltown Boy stands at the bar, T-shirt and jeans hanging from a skinny frame that makes him look younger than his seventeen years. No frocks for him but, like a casual-wear Cinderella, he's made it to the ball all the same. He blew into the big city less than a month ago, stepping off the bus with all the dreams and hopes of a wannabe Hollywood starlet alighting from a Greyhound in the City of Angels. He's doing well, got himself a manager, and he's already a face in the piano bar. Three weeks in and he's still hanging onto his dreams. Cynicism hasn't got a chokehold on his heart—not yet.

The wannabe starlets dream of silver screen fame, red carpet success. Smalltown Boy's dreams are vague. He has misty notions of making it. He doesn't know what "making it" means, except that he'll be living in an apartment—not a flat, *apartment* sounds fancier—and when he stands in front of the floor-to-ceiling windows, a vista of the city will be laid out before him like he's King of the World. An apartment where everything is clean and doesn't smell of mildew like the squat his manager's set him up in.

He knows that it will come, that everything will fall into place just like he knew his luck would change the moment he left home. And so, it did. Feet barely hitting the pavement, still sucking in bus fumes, and he'd already got himself a manager. More like the manager got *him*. Spotted him on the street, saw his potential straightaway. "Gotta place to stay, kid?"

So now he's got a place in a squat and—aside from the damp on the walls and no hot water—it's not too bad, kind of nice really, and he's got his manager, and his manager knows how it works here and he sees the potential in Smalltown boy and Smalltown Boy still has his dreams.

A drag queen draped in emerald green is teasing Smalltown Boy at the bar when a night-tripper arrives. The tourist is dressed in a 9-to-5 suit, briefcase in hand. Real leather, not vinyl. The suit's a cut above, didn't come off the rack at C&A. His shirt collar is crisp and white, ironed by the wife who made his toast that morning before waving him off from suburbia with a "*Have a good day at the office, dear.*" She thinks he's working late. Wining and dining an important client. It's an excuse he's used before and she always believes him. She has no reason for suspicion. There have been no tells. He never brings home the lingering scent of another woman, no lipstick on the collar.

The beauty of it is, there is no lie: He did wine and dine a client that evening and on all the other evenings, too, so if his late nights ever come up at the annual office do—the one the wives are invited to—she'll only ever hear what she already knows. The lie is in the omission of what comes after the wining and dining and the client and Briefcase Man have parted ways.

A subtle nod speaks volumes in a thronging Soho bar. Emerald Green notes the exchange between Briefcase Man and Smalltown Boy's manager. Pimp, more like. She wonders at the boy's naivety, wonders if he's using yet. She slides from her stool and, as she sashays to the piano, she thinks about how she'd like to help the boy.

Briefcase Man and the manager walk to the side of the bar to speak, but only for a moment. Briefcase Man is a regular, comes to the piano bar after every wining and dining of a client, which averages out at once a month, more or less. He knows the drill and the manager knows his tastes. He likes the new boys. The ones fresh off the bus from Nowheresville. There's no need to waste conversation over the transaction.

The exchange of words and cash is swift and understated. Briefcase Man goes to the back of the bar, exits through the door marked **Toilets**. Smalltown Boy follows. At the piano, Emerald Green ripples out the opening chords of "I Will Survive."

Three weeks in and Smalltown Boy's knees are once more grinding against the cubicle floor, grime chafing into his jeans, mouth full of cock and still hanging onto his dreams. Briefcase Man grunts, grabs a handful of Smalltown Boy's hair, forcing his dick deeper into the boy's mouth. Smalltown Boy's eyes are closed tight, his manager's words playing in his head: *"Nobody makes it overnight. You gotta get yourself known and, while you're doing that, you gotta make a living, boy."*

Smalltown Boy likes the piano bar, there's movie glitz in its 1950s décor. And the drag queens—especially Emerald Green—are nice to him, but he can't see how blowing off these old guys in their suits is going to help him make it. He can't figure out how a bellyful of spunk is going to get him out of the squat.

His manager disagrees. *"Where do you think all those big stars got their breaks? On their knees, that's where."*

Smalltown Boy thinks about the Hollywood melodramas his mother used to watch and about the most glamourous woman in them. He asks his manager if the same is true of Joan Crawford.

"*Are you kidding me?*" His manager laughs and makes the tongue-in-cheek blowjob gesture, his hand moving back and fore in front of his mouth.

Smalltown Boy thinks that if the Queen of Hollywood started on her knees, then so can he.

Briefcase Man makes a weird noise when he cums, a choking wheeze, like he's the one with old man meat stuck in his throat. He judders and Smalltown Boy wonders if the old bastard is having a heart attack or a stroke.

But then he's pushed away, jizz dribbling down his chin as Briefcase Man does himself up, straightens himself out, and grabs his briefcase from the top of the cistern. He's out of there, in a rush to catch the train back to suburbia. He knows his wife will be waiting up for him, keeping company with a glass of chardonnay and Friday night TV. "*How was your day, dear? Are you tired?*"

She has no idea what he does all week long in the city. Something important. Something to do with moving money around, but she understands very well what he does with his precious spare time. He's the chairman of the Neighborhood Watch (got to keep the riffraff out), treasurer of the local Rotary Club, an educated man, a respected man who does good deeds. She's proud of the fact that he's a regular Pillar of the Community.

He doesn't think about her when he's riding the train home. He's thinking about Smalltown Boy, about the contours of his skull and how it felt in his hand. He's thinking about the easy grabbing of Smalltown Boy's thick hair. About the way his young mouth slid so smoothly up and down the shaft of Briefcase Man's dick. He's thinking he'd like to fuck the boy before he becomes dead in the eyes like all the others.

Smalltown Boy rinses his mouth and cleans off his face at the sink. He thinks he'll order a Coke when he goes back to the bar. Take away the taste. He's got a tab open. His manager takes care of the bill. His manager takes care of all his expenses, including his share of the squat. Smalltown Boy always thought squats were free. "*Rent-free but you still gotta pay the rates and the electric and that mattress didn't cost nothing.*" Everything has a price, him included. Trouble is, by the time all his expenses are taken care of, there's not much left and, somehow, even though he sucks a lot of cock, he feels a little bit further away from making it with every punter.

"*Need a little something to take the edge off?*"

He's declined, so far. He might not know much, but he knows that if he starts using, his manager will add it to his expenses and, before he knows it, he'll be owing the manager money instead of the other way around. Three weeks in and it already feels like his manager owns him. Smalltown Boy goes back through to the bar, thinking he maybe won't have that Coke after all. He can barely afford to eat as it is and doesn't need the expense. He wonders if there're any calories in sperm but thinks there can't be because he's had his fill and his ribs persist in sticking out.

Emerald Green is still at the piano, the gathered crowd swaying and joining in with her soulful rendition of "Over the Rainbow." One of the other drag queens dabs away a tear. Smalltown Boy thinks Emerald Green is the most beautiful person he's ever seen. An exotic angel. He can't imagine her in a place reeking of mildew or sleeping on a mattress on the floor, and he thinks that he'd like to live with her. That she would look after him and spoil him and that he could look after her, too. Do nice things for her. Rub her shoulders when she's tired, like he used to do for his mother. Tidy up and make cups of tea. And he'd make her laugh. He likes it when Emerald Green laughs and he likes it even better when she smiles at him.

Right at the moment when he's thinking it, she looks in his direction. She's singing but her eyes smile at him, making him feel warm inside. He wants to go stand with the group at the piano. He wants to sing and sway with them and maybe dab away a tear or two, though, why he feels like crying, he doesn't know. It's only been three weeks, after all.

The first week was the toughest. He'd never sucked a cock before. Where he comes from, that kind of thing can get you beat up and left for dead. It wasn't just the punters who were tough though—it was everything all at once. The city's so big, so full of people who his manager needs to protect him from. "*Stick with me and you'll be fine.*"

It's exciting and terrifying at the same time and he's struggling to get his head around it all. Amid the chaos, being in the presence of Emerald Green soothes him. Her voice soars. Smalltown Boy dabs away a tear and wonders why he's crying.

That's something else that would get him beat up and left for dead back at home. *Sissy boy.*

Three weeks and he's lost count of the cocks he's had in his mouth. Maybe he could figure it out if he tried but the punters merge one into the other. It's only the bad ones that stick out, the ones that stink, and the gross fat ones with bellies that hang down like blubbery aprons, and the really old ones with papery skin and cocks that don't get properly hard. They never come, and fuck, his jaws ache after blowing them. He remembers the kind ones too, but there're not many of those so it isn't much of a challenge. To the rest, he's just a mouth to be bought. Even so, he's hanging on to his dreams.

Smalltown Boy's neck prickles. His manager is looking at him. Speaking without opening his mouth. There's a man standing beside him. An old fat man. The old fat man is also looking at Smalltown Boy. The tip of the old fat man's tongue oozes from his mouth and swipes his lips. The old fat man nods and then he and the manager make the sleight of hand deal.

The old fat man goes through the door marked **toilets** and Smalltown Boy follows. He doesn't know that Emerald Green is watching him through the cigarette haze. He doesn't know that she's thinking about him even as he gets down on his knees and prays. He doesn't know that she's singing a new song, that she's singing it for him.

Author Bio

Twitter: @LGThomson1   Instagram: @L.G.Thomson

LG Thomson is an artist of many mediums, living in Ullapool, a fishing village in the Scottish Highlands lying on the same latitude as Lost Cove, Alaska. Her writing has appeared in a range of publications including *Wyldblood Magazine, Epoch Press,* Anxiety Press' *Elegies in the Dust,* Urban Pigs Press' *Hunger,* and Craig Clevenger's *Diner Noir.*

Thomson is the author of seven novels, including neo-noir thriller *Boyle's Law.* She also released two searingly honest and brutally funny to touching memoirs with Outcast Press about growing up in Scotland's experimental New Town and going to art school in Glasgow's punk scene.

More From Our Authors

Compulsive Swim is Austin Davis's second illustrated poetry book from Outcast Press, with brief pieces just as rock 'n' roll and emotional but structured like play acts. There's longing, philosophizing and eulogizing but written as accessibly as street graffiti, with a slight romance to the cold grit and grime like a Nirvana song.

"Davis holds in his hands an understanding for the diversity of emotion like it's the fragile globe of a dandelion ready for wishes." – Caitie Young, *The Poetry Question*

Perv Tax

By Mark Burrow

Tracey Clarke sits on the roof of the garages. She throws stones at a **No Ball Games** sign attached to the end wall of a block of flats. I freeze when I realize she's spotted me, feelin' the fear that Junior an' her idiot boyfriend, Robert, are nearby. Those two are always wantin' to dish out beatings.

"Hi, Jay," she says.

"Alright," I reply. "What you doin'?"

"Nothing much," she says.

"How come you're not at school?" I say, tryin' not to be obvious lookin' at her skinny white legs danglin' over the side.

"Didn't feel like it today."

"Oh."

"What about you?" she asks.

"What?"

"School."

"They gave us the afternoon off."

"What for?"

"Some random was shootin' into classrooms with an air rifle from the flats across the road."

She does her deep an' dirty laugh. "What, shooting into the school?"

"Through the open windows. We had to get on our bellies an' crawl outta class."

"That's crazy."

"Yeah."

"So, where you going?" she asks.

I know I should lie but I kinda fancy Tracey an' do the stupidest thing ever by tellin' her the truth. I say, "I've got a key to the roof of the tower block, so I was goin' up there to chill."

"No way."

I struggle to get the words out, but I manage to say, "Do you wanna come?"

"Deffo." She hangs off the roof an' drops to the ground. "Let's go," she says.

We walk together, side by side. It feels like I'm trippin' on the shroom wine Mum's girlfriend makes, cos how can I be walking with Tracey fucken Clarke?

My heart is poundin' in my chest as if I've been runnin' a hundred miles per hour. I don't get how bein' with a girl can make your insides flip over like it's Pancake Day. It's nuts cos me an' her ain't talkin' about much either. Well, to be fair, I'm not talkin' at all. Tracey's the one chattin' an' acting like she wants us to be friends. When it's my turn to chat, I get that buffering in my head that only happens with girls an' maths.

We pass the playground where nobody plays an' I get nervous cos normally I go the long way round to reach the front entrance of the tower block. Going this way, it's too easy to be spotted by fools who hang around by the swings, listenin' to lame music an' smokin' fat spliffs.

"I'm goin' to see my bro tomorrow," I say.

"Mike?"

"Yeah."

"Mike's alright."

"It freaks me out a bit."

"What does?"

"Seein' my bro in prison."

"It's not prison, though, is it?" she asks. "Didn't he go to Young Offenders? I've been there on visits. I don't mind it."

"What about the smell?"

She does her laugh. "What do you care about smell? Young Offenders is just school with fake guards."

"I suppose."

"Can I ask you a question?" says Tracey.

"Go for it," I say, seein' we're coming to the front of the tower block.

"How come you were perving on me?"

It's like she's gone an' macheted me in the guts. "I wasn't," I sort of shout back at her.

"Yeah, a couple of weeks ago, you totally were."

"When?"

"I was snogging Robert— What did you throw a bottle at us for?"

"I never."

"You did. Why'd you fling it?"

"I didn't."

"Liar."

"Nah, nah."

"Yeah, yeah."

I start stuttering, sayin', "I, I, I," an' I wonder why she's turnin' on me an' sounding all gangsta. I ain't no spy or one of those creepy-creep men who pay to see Mum. Alright, I do watch Tracey on the estate now an' then. I was lyin' flat on the roof of the garages once, silent as a spider, listenin' to her tell Robert that her grandad's ghost haunts her nan's flat an' that she woke up one night an' saw a whiteness floatin' across the room, an' she knew it was her grandad, an' she was frightened outta her mind an', when she tried to holler, nothin' came out. She says the room went proper cold.

I like how she laughs, Tracey Clarke, 'cept when she cracks up at me when I'm getting' slagged off for the holes in my tops, my no-name trainers, greasy hair, an' everyone findin' out about Mum's webcam stuff. Fools gettin' snidey, sayin' Mum finishes work when she gets outta bed. Nah, nah, not funny at all. They say I smell rank an' I never get invited in no one's flat ever cos their mums think I'm from a bad family an' it's as if we have germs that are gunna infect their stupid flats an' I don't have friends, not really, never have, an' that's okay by me. I don't want none anyway.

Tracey swivels an' walks backwards, sayin', "You can't tell me, can you? You can't because you know you were perving at us like the little grot you are."

"I wasn't."

An' we both know I'm telling lies an' that I did throw a slate—not a bottle—cos I couldn't stand watchin' her kiss that idiot.

I clock she's lookin' behind me.

I turn round an' there they are, Junior an' Dong Head. They're too close for me to run.

They grab hold of me, yankin' off my rucksack.

I must scream an' shout really loud cos Tracey does the dirtiest laugh.

"He's got the key to the tower block roof," she says. "Let's take him up there."

They're having the best time. Robert squeezes my arm tight. "Don't think about running," he says.

I'm tryin' hard not to blub.

Tracey says stuff like, "It's the tax you have to pay for being such a perv."

"Perv tax," says Junior, takin' out a plastic thing to scan open the heavy door with wired glass to enter the tower block.

I never realized he lived here. We stand an' wait for a lift. I keep hopin' we see a policeman or someone who can save me.

The lift doors open an' we step inside.

Junior presses the button.

The whole lift has been tagged. It's a spaghetti of reds, yellows, greens, silvers, an' blues.

Tracey looks at Robert grippin' me an' says to him, "You best wash your hands after."

"I know," he says an', to me, he goes, "Guess what?"

I say, "What?"

"You stink."

Tracey does a scum bucket laugh. I don't like it one little bit anymore. It's so loud an' fake. Seriously, nothin' is that funny.

Junior says, "Why don't you wash?"

"Don't you have soap?" asks Robert.

"Haven't you seen his mum?" says Tracey.

"Yeah," says Robert, "she's a proper nasty skank."

Junior gets close to me an' goes, "Say it."

"Say what?"

"Don't 'what' me. Who you chatting to?"

Robert squeezes my arm tighter an' goes, "Say: My mum's a skank."

"Fuck off," I shout at them.

"You best say it," says Tracey.

So, I look into Robert's piglet eyes an' go, "Your mum's a skank."

Junior an' Tracey give each other these *oh-my-gosh* looks.

Robert slaps my face. "Who do you think you're fucking talking to? You think we're playing? You think this is games?"

My cheek goes mega hot.

He slaps me again.

The lift stops an' the doors slide open.

"Get the key," says Tracey.

Junior searches my pockets, sayin', "I'm gunna catch diseases putting my hands in here."

I really wanna blub. I wish I was at home in my room. On my bed, travelin' back in time to when my bro would be on the other bed an' I'd hear him tell his funny stories, makin' me laugh so much I couldn't breathe.

Junior has the key an' he unlocks the noisy steel door to the roof. Robert drags me, tellin' me to move, but I don't want to go up the stairs.

"You're gunna get it," says Junior.

Robert keeps slappin' my head like I'm a fucken bongo. I can see how angry he is for me cussing his mum, who I now remember is dead or some kind of root vegetable in a home after overdosin' or somethin' druggy an' grim. We step onto the roof an' the sunlight makes us blink.

Junior tips my rucksack. A can of Dr Pepper rolls along the concrete floor. He rummages in the bag an' sees a pack of fags, a lighter an' a spliff. He offers them to Robert an' Tracey.

They're not bothered so he lights my spliff for himself an' pockets the pack an' lighter cos that's the kind of budget thief he is an' always will be.

Robert shoves me down an' kicks me.

It hurts an' I can feel the tears comin' like sad traffic cos I know no one is rescuin' me up here.

Tracey says, "That's what you get for perving."

Without shame, Junior cracks open my Dr Pepper an' starts drinkin'.

Tracey an' Junior think this is jokes. Robert don't. It's the mum cuss that's got him pumped. There's some random rule about not cussin' dead mums when it's okay to cuss my mum. Me an' my big mouth. I never know when to keep it shut. There's this teacher, Mr. Leonard, who says I'm a foul-mouthed youth an' I reckon he ain't wrong neither. Either. I've made Robert mad an' I'm fucken scared. Some people, right, they go *wah-wah* crazy on booze an' drugs. Others don't need to take no nothin'. Psycho is their bassline.

"He's crying," says Tracey.

"Fucking baby," goes Junior, doin' a Dr Pepper burp.

Robert says, "No one's disrespecting me these ways." He pulls me up an' then lifts me, squeezin' me tight. He carries me to the side of the tower block roof.

I feel myself getting closer. I start to freak.

He's too strong. I wriggle an' worm to free myself but he plops me on the edge, grabbin' my legs, an' he pushes me backwards so I'm hangin' over.

I feel the distance below. I see how the veins twitch in Robert's neck an' how red his face is goin'. I'm heavier than he thought. He's strainin'. Teeth showin'. Zits about to pop. Any second, I'm gunna slip from his hands.

My head goes dizzy from upside-down-seeing the flatness of the tower block, all 14 stories, window after window, laddering to the ground, where I'm gunna land an' burst open like fried tomatoes.

Robert says, "Tell me: What's your mum?" There are frothy bubbles an' strings of spit on his mouth from strugglin' to keep his grip.

Tracey's chantin', "Say it. Say it. Say it."

I'm a witch they want to burn.

I'm the egg boy, ready to crack.

Blood rushes to my head.

The key to where I live falls outta my pocket. I watch it tumble downwards, spinnin' an' turnin' down, down, down... The windows explode. It's a deafenin' sound like when a chandelier drops an' crashes in a movie.

I wait a second an' then the cryin' starts. The tower block's tears stream out. It's the sadness of all the tenants in the flats, of my dad havin' to run away, of Mike beatin' up the stranger who pushed in at a bus stop an' him bein' sent to Young Offenders, of the muggin's, the rapes, the stabbin's, the crackies an' the alkies. The way the men smack up women, the borin' schools with depressed coffee-breath teachers, the angry bus drivers. The no jobs, the do-nothing no-nothing days, the old ladies who die all alone cos they don't have enough money for the fags an' the gin they need to make them feel less lonely. It's my mum scammin' duh-brain meatheads with their hard-ons an' spunk.

It's the estate fucken hatin' being an estate. It's the signs for **No Ball Games** an' **No Dogs** an' **Keep off the Grass** that wish they were better signs like the pukka one on the motorway that tells drivers they can stamp the accelerator to go turbo. It's me, cos I hate it here an' havin' to be the ghost spider. It's the people. It's what I am an' what I ain't an' the not knowin' what I'll ever be.

I feel the tower twistin' for sure. Tears bulgin' from hundreds of windows. The panes of glass shatterin' an' droplets splashin' down onto the streets below, floodin' the ground-floor flats, the water risin' up, cos it don't stop cryin', the tower block. It has seen too much, heard the sadness inside, deep in its pipes an' plumbin', felt the pain buttered across the years, that dead-end grimness of all the beatin's an suicidin's that go on an' on an' on.

Water spunkin' through the streets. Washing away the dogshit an' the rats an' the burnt cars.

Hands reachin' out. Tattooed desperados who wanna be saved.

Nah, nah, that ain't happening.

They're drownin' in a warm sea of salty tower block tears.

An' yeah, I'm blubbin' too, 'cept the tears are going backwards, reversin' up my temples an' forehead an' into my hair, an' I hear a voice shout, "My mum's a skank. My mum's a skank. My mum's a..."

"...Fucking dirty skank," says Robert, heavin' me back up.

Gravity softens as soon as half my body is back on the roof. Robert lets go an' I pull the rest of me to safety.

He coughs an' gobs. "Spliff," he says to Junior.

I'm on my knees, retchin'.

Tracey is in stitches. "That's the funniest thing I ever saw," she says to Robert.

This roof was my safe place. It's where I could come an' hide out from the evils, where I could chill in the summer, staring at the fluffy clouds, watchin' the crucifix airplanes an' imagine I was with dad like when he used to bring me up here, lookin' at the whole skyline of the city, the two of us on top of the world, talkin' about the foreign places we could travel to an' see.

Part of me is cryin' cos I won't be coming up here again.

Robert catches me reachin' for the key by my rucksack an' he stomps my hand. "What do you think you're doing?" he says, squishin' my fingers.

"Stop it," I yell.

"Your whole family is disgusting," he says, lookin' at the snot dribbling from my nose.

"Gross," says Tracey, starin' at me like I'm an alien.

"Get him out of here," says Robert to Junior.

"You should've dropped him," says Tracey.

"I still can," he says, draggin' on the last of the spliff.

"Come on," says Junior an' he helps me to my feet an' takes me across the roof an' down the stairs.

We go through the squeaky metal door. Junior's not laughin' or actin like he's gunna do more damages. It's as if he changes into someone else the second that he's away from Tracey an' Robert.

Quietly, he says, "Sorry, bruv, that was harsh." He presses the button for the lift. "You best go home, you knows... Stay low." He gives me my fags an' lighter. He seems like he's gunna speak again but stops himself.

I watch him close an' lock the hefty door, goin' back onto the roof.

My roof.

AuthOr BiO

Twitter: @MarkBurrow20   Instagram: @MarkBurrow24

Mark Burrow, who lives in Brighton, UK, has published the novella, *Coo*, through Alien Buddha Press. It's about an alcoholic turning into a pigeon in a world where failed DJs become swans and the insane transform into birds of prey.

Burrow's "Perv Tax" was originally published in *Punk Noir Magazine's* Hellton Towers edition and is a chapter of his novel in progress. Sections of such also appear in *Underbelly Press, Frazzled Lit,* and Urban Pigs Press' *Hunger* anthology.

More From Our Authors

Punk Noir Magazine is a popular website that specializes in crime fiction, ranging from micros and flashes to poetry and monthly short story prompts hosted by different guest editors. The likes of such have included James Jenkins for the Hell in a High-Rise theme.

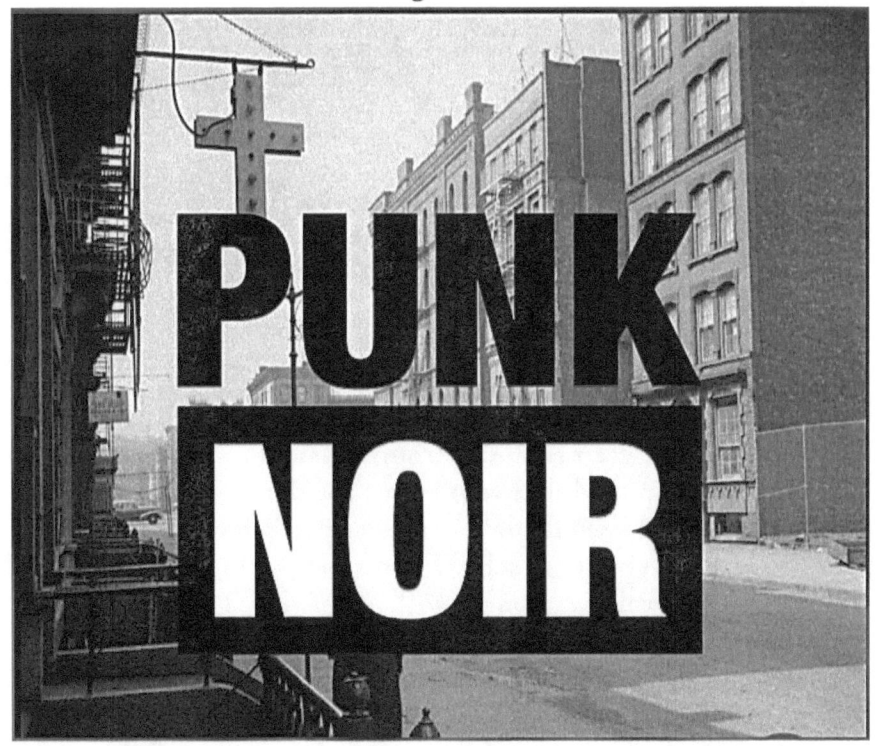

Run by Outcast Press authors Stephen J. Golds (*In Filth It Shall Be Found, Diner Noir, Half-Empty Doorways*, and *Shadows Slow Dancing in Derelict Rooms*) and B F Jones (*The Edge of Nowhere*), look for them at www.PunkNoirMagazine.Wordpress.com

Deprivation Of Character

By Jeff Schneider

If I could re-do college, I would pay less attention to my lab partner, who was originally from Russia and enthusiastically dissected a fetal pig while I took notes for the two of us. I would ignore all this and I would devote more time to having dirty sex.

I was too young, in school, and stuck with the basics: some drunken nights rolling around with someone. Then there were the Christmas breaks where I ████ my townie ex. He never changed. He performed the same routine of ████████, then licking his way up to my ██, biting my neck (which was when I got excited), and then manipulating me into ████ style, ████████ within seconds. Hometown rallies never change.

Now I'm 30 and somehow living with a man who has a substantial Funko Pops collection on a shelf behind his gaming domain. Things like this make me sad. We have freedom, he isn't all bad—so he says.

The talks at his Wednesday night poker games over at Brad's house are animated. He certainly describes things he's done to me with vigor, I am sure. His Lego collection never comes up at times like this. We have done about as much as two people can do with the pegs and holes we were given. The morals our parents imposed on us as children are what we're destroying under the sheets and in the shower.

Pregnancy is not an option. Relationship goals in general are small. He is making money and I am creating art. My thing has always been collage. In my studio, there are piles of finished work, human dissection collages and ancient skull collages and full moon collages. My attraction to the macabre is not lost in any of my pieces. Then there are the scrap piles raked up into corners of the space like leaves. The rejected images always remind me of ██.

Just the way he would never eat my ██ or anything resembling kink. He was scrap most of the time, in fact, *all* of the time in bed. Although, we were still pretty good-looking. Everything appeared acceptable and on course, yet there was something always missing.

This was when the accident happened. I was driving home from a night at Tina's place, where she and I always chatted about books, played board games, drank wine, and bitched about ██████. Tina didn't have sex problems. She made a three-figure salary in sex-work. One time, I was at her place when she was with a client. He paid extra just because he thought I watched her ██████ him off, but I didn't, my mind was focused on jealous thoughts about her finances. I stirred my tea cup, the spoon dinging the insides. The sound made him ██ fast, even though my intent was elsewhere.

This night though, I was quite sloshed. She poured the Alizé generously. She danced around with her high-cut sweat-shorts that said ██ on her ██ while I sat and drank. When the energy faded, I told myself I was okay to drive and refused the Uber she was ordering. It was foggy and dark this night and, in terror, I almost hit a person coming around the corner.

He was changing his flat tire on the shoulder of this two-lane byway. He foolishly had a black coat on—idiot, he was invisible. My tires screeched as I swerved to avoid him.

I looked back in the mirror and he was leaning down, his jack tipped over on the road.

My heart raced, worrying that I'd killed him.

Turning around, I was scared and all I could hear was the sand grinding under my tires in the ten points that it took to turn and go back his way. I was terrified about the fact that I was indeed quite drunk. My mind raced with thoughts of Tina and her success, and how I was just fucking up all over the place.

Once my headlights hit his body, I could see he was fine, standing there with his hands out, signaling like, *What the fuck?*

I rolled up next to him and said something like, "I am so, so, sorry."

He walked up to my window and looked me in the eyes, then took a step back.

This was when I saw how cute he was.

I asked if he needed a ride and he accepted.

He threw the jack away from his truck as if he'd never return to fix the thing at all.

We exchanged niceties following the directions to the gas station. I got a text from my partner that asked, **Staying the night?** with a heart emoji.

I didn't reply.

The guy said, "You know what? Fuck my truck. Can you drive me to a hotel? That thing is more work than I can deal with tonight. I'll call someone in the morning."

Probably too enthusiastically, I replied, "Sure."

We drove to the local motel frequented by transients and truckers. It was the only place I knew of that was near the highway in case I needed to get home.

We pulled up and he got out right away. He walked over to my window again and leaned down to look in. He said, "Why don't you park and come in?"

My urge was to quiver and explain, make a fool out of myself, and somehow get back into my passive safety zone, yet something came over me like a wave, a warm Caribbean wave from my spine forward, over my skull and into my eyes. And on some paranoid level, it made sense to comply with whatever this guy wanted than to get the cops involved with a drunk driving accident.

But I just said, "Why?"

The guy leaned in more and smiled a cute, coy smile. He said, "So we can make this night better. I am dirty, but I think tonight, if you don't mind, I'll keep it that way."

I parked and walked with him.

I decided to hold his hand on the way in. As it was cold, I put his hand in my back pocket.

He responded by grabbing my ███. It was not a loving rub, but more of a fondle, something I would regularly be outraged by, but I committed to see how much I could push things tonight.

I needed more.

Rather than ripping off my clothes in the room, he sat in the office chair and started asking me questions—all sorts of perverted questions—right away.

I took off my clothes as he sat there, ████████ ██████ through his jeans.

I got down on my knees and ██████ him.

He pushed me onto the bed and took off his clothes as well. He ████████ me and put his other hand near my mouth.

I sucked his middle finger. When I touched him, he was very ████.

He asked me to lay on my stomach and ██████████ as he ██████ my ███.

He rode me in all positions and I █████████ twice.

He was still ████ ████.

It was then that he asked me for what he called, "the bad way," which I knew from watching ████ to be ██ ███ ███.

I didn't respond but took his wrist and guided his hand there from where it was on my █████ so he could touch it.

I was ███ and he spit on my ███, █████████ the ███. Eventually, I pushed back, allowing his finger to enter with a groan. It hurt but I wanted the pain and to swim in the humiliation. I arched my back to let him go deeper. I loudly moaned as his fingers went deep up my █████ ███████.

He bent my leg forward and, at that point, had two ███████ in. I was riding them and vigorously playing with ██ ████.

I reached back and guided his ████ to my ███████.

He was excited, I could tell, panting like a leopard. He slowly positioned himself and left it up to me to push back on his soldier.

He went up my ███ and I let out a concerned moan, in slight ████, shock, and embarrassment.

I wanted more and more of this feeling.

I pushed my other leg upward, showing him a full view of my ███, myself bent over, and began to slowly ride him. My ███

hung down and, as I rocked back and forth, they followed with a slight delay.

I grunted with painful pleasure, letting out real whimpers for mercy, not the porn-like ones Tina would make when she was working. As he pulled out and repeatedly entered my ████████, I felt like a true █████ and he told me I was one.

This role, I became fully.

Soon, he was ██████ me at a good pace.

I cried out in a high pitch and put my head down, feeling the shame. I thought of how unbelievable this was. I wanted to be a dirty little █████. I wanted to ████ him afterwards just to be disgusting.

He was ██████ and ██████ until he was ready to ████████.

I pushed off of him, as I didn't want him to ███ up my ███. While I played with my ███, I reached through my legs with my other hand and █████ him ███. I could tell my ████████ was █████ and I pushed out a small ████ that fell on the bed.

I had another ██████.

This seemed to excite him very much, as if a reward was given. He ████ on my open ████ immediately.

We breathed heavy and fell to our sides, laughing.

He got up quickly and cleaned off the bed with a towel from the bathroom. He wiped my ███ with a facecloth.

We lay in silence with dazed looks on our faces.

Quite soon, he was snoring and I cleaned up in the bathroom and left.

On my way home, I felt magical.

Yet I did not want moments of ecstatic disgust like the one I just engaged in to enter my relationship. I hid this dirty pleasure in a special place.

I have the best ███████ thinking about that accidental night.

AuthOr BiO

Twitter: @PigPublishing   Instagram: @PigRoastPublishing

Jeff Schneider from Providence, Rhode Island, is a published writer and guitarist in the noise-rock groups Arab On Radar and Made in Mexico. He is the author of the memoir *Psychiatric Tissues: The Arab On Radar Book*, a collection of short stories titled *Gallons Per Minute*, and the novel *Therapists Gone Wild*. He also has a forthcoming novel titled *Rockin Out on the Mainline*.

Schneider is the editor in chief of the outsider literary press Pig Roast Publishing, LLC. They specialize in books about underground art and music.

WOrmS

By James Jenkins

Dee allowed the punter to drone on. A welcome distraction from the baggy skin loosely held together by brittle bones and sinew. At least he was clean—physically. The old veck prattled on about his previous life. The one before he was forced to visit girls of the night.

Dee didn't mind, the talkers were easy money. It was the quiet types you had to watch—hair-pulling, choking, punching. Too costly in her line of work. She toyed with the idea of pulling a can of "spesh" from her little fridge but decided against it. What if he asked for one? It was too late to run to the store. Instead, Dee tried to focus on the man's story.

An old sci-fi movie, about to be massacred with a remake. He was pleading like she possessed the power to pull the fucking plug on it. Something, something David fucking Lynch! The way the man preached, you'd think it was God himself. Most was filtered out by her practiced patience. *Most.*

"You don't understand. People your age just want CGI, it's all computer graphics."

It wasn't that Dee didn't understand—She just didn't give a fuck; he wasn't paying her to listen.

"Where's the real art? Back in my day, we made all the effects ourselves. Beautiful, time-consuming works of love. *I. Me.* Goddammit, I built those fucking worms and for what?! To be torn up and re-sweat out by some nerd on a computer."

He sat up, anger giving life to those old bones, and she spotted his leathery prick swelling with blood.

"Your hour's up. You need to pay for anything else."

He looked down, surprised at his stamina. Staring at the one-eyed viper as if it was about to strike him right on the nose. "Well, I'll be damned. I haven't had two boners in the same day for a decade now. You're good, ain't you, girl?"

Dee knew she couldn't take the credit. The old boy had been harping on about himself and his worms for the last ten minutes. That wasn't going to stop her making an extra $50. Dee would exercise this fossilized piece of man flesh one more time and not even have to leave her bed to find another client.

The man reached for his folded corduroys and pulled out a handful of notes. He knew the drill. He paused. "I'd like to try something else..."

"Look, guy, I don't do no pissing, shitting, or gagging, okay?"

No reply. Instead, he swung his legs off the bed.

Dee watched the varicose veins throb to life as he crossed the room for his briefcase.

With a wry smile, he placed it upon her coffee table and snapped it open. "You must come across some sick bastards. Nothing like that. How about toys?"

Dee relaxed with a seductive smile, her polished act back on. Toys were okay. That meant more than the base pay. "Whatcha got for me, baby?"

He carefully removed two cylindrical objects, a couple inches thick and six long. He delicately held them in each hand with a pincher grip.

"Butt plugs?" Dee laughed. "No problem. Are they for you or me?"

"Oh, these are for you, sweetheart."

"Okay, but it's an extra $50 on top." Easy money. She'd had worse—much worse.

The old man burrowed through the notes, extracting more than the agreed fee. "Some extra if I can finish on your back?"

"You got it, honey," said Dee. Very easy money. She'd have let him do that for free. Dee climbed onto the bed, all fours, sticking her arse up in expectation.

The man shuffled up fully to attention. He fed in the first.

Dee couldn't feel much. This wasn't her first rodeo.

"I spent my life working on these little beauties. All my time dedicated to designing, developing, building—testing—them." He guided the second one in.

Dee was beginning to feel a twitching inside her lower stomach.

"My legacy! Replaced with a glorified fucking cartoon!"

Dee was restless now. One hand cradled her belly. They lashed around inside her.

"But I can't allow that. No. Their legacy, *my* legacy. It will live on."

Dee's other hand collapsed, bringing the rest of her down onto the bed. She usually added an extra tenner for each inch above average. If she made it through, then she'd be charging him pain tax. The pain was nearing impossible.

"Relax, girl. It won't take long."

Dee couldn't scream through the blood that choked her. Her limbs violently thrashed at her own body. Determined to reach inside and pull the beasties out.

He was right—It didn't take long.

The worms left the tortured corpse, burrowing their way out for the man to collect.

He placed them both back in the suitcase and dressed.

His liver-spotted hand retrieved the girl's payment.

A drop of fresh blood transferred onto the well-used notes and mixed with all the others. A forensic wet dream.

Before he left, he placed a movie poster on the body. "Let's see whose worms are on tomorrow's front page."

AuthOr BiO

Instagram: @James_Jenkins_Writer

James Jenkins lives in Ipswich, UK, with his wife and children. He is a writer of gritty realism, dark humor, and noir. His debut novel *Parochial Pigs* is available on Amazon. This started a trilogy now published through Anxiety Press. The two sequels are titled *Sun Bleached Scarecrows* and *The Swine, The Pig & The Porker.*

Jenkins is the co-founder of Urban Pigs Press (UrbanPigsPress.Co.UK), which produced the food bank-supporting charity anthology *Hunger*. He may also sometimes feature as guest editor for *Punk Noir Magazine.*

Lot Lizard

By JD Clapp

I stopped for gas and a cold drink near the turnoff for the Mojave National Preserve on old highway 395. My truck's external thermometer read 111 Fahrenheit. Dry heat or not, it was fucking hot. I put 80 bucks in the tank then parked near the door to the minimart. A young woman—maybe that was being generous—a *girl* walked toward me from the shady side of the building. She followed me in.

"Hey, there. You heading to Bakersfield?" she asked.

I looked back. She wore cut-off jean shorts, a skimpy white tank top, her pink lace bra showing through. She shuffled her dirty feet in flip flops that looked two sizes too big. I wondered, *Lot lizard or runaway?*

Trouble either way.

"No. Sorry. I'm heading northeast, up to Bishop."

"Buy me a cold drink? It's hot out here."

My gut told me to brush her off, but I decided this might be a chance to do something decent for somebody. I'd learned over a series of fuck-ups that doing good deeds, even small ones, were steps away from whatever hole I'd put myself in.

"Sure. What do you want?" I asked.

She walked past me to the beer cooler, opened it, and bent over like she was looking for something on the bottom shelf, the bottom of her ass cheeks popping free of her shorts. She looked back over her shoulder and smiled. Then she stood up and took a tallboy of Miller Lite from the singles rack at her eye-level. "Ah, here they are. I'll have one of these."

I smirked. *Really subtle there. That answers that.* Lot lizard. "You even 21?" I asked.

"I'm 22. Totally legal...or anything." She handed me the can, then held on to it for a split second, and looked me in the eye. "Thanks, handsome," she said.

"22, eh? Same age as my daughter." My daughter who was not speaking to me and would be disco mad that I was buying a working girl a beer.

She gave me a pouty little frown.

I picked up some pretzels, a bag of beef jerky, and a Diet Coke for myself. I paid the clerk, who looked at me, then back to the girl, clearly annoyed.

Outside, I handed the lot lizard her brew, and climbed into my truck.

"Can I catch a ride to Ridgecrest?" she asked. "I can't pay for gas, but we can work something out..."

Again, my gut screamed, *Don't do it!* But where had my gut gotten me besides a three-week bender in L.A.?

"Get in," I said.

She smiled. "Hold on for a sec." She moved as quickly as she could in those jumbo flip-flops, almost tripping as she ducked back around the side of the building.

Great. Now what?

She re-emerged with a backpack and a chocolate lab/pit bull puppy tied to a makeshift rope leash.

And here we go.

She tossed her pack in the truck bed with my stuff, opened the passenger door, hoisted the puppy onto the seat, and climbed in. "This is Buster," she said, patting the dog's head.

She popped open her beer, took a swig, then ran the can across her forehead. "Damn, it's hot... I'm Hailey, by the way."

"I'm Jim. Nice to meet you," I said.

The puppy whined a little and she rubbed his belly, shushed him. "Listen, thanks again for the ride. Let's get business out of the way. I'll give you a handy and take my top off to pay for the ride. Or I'll blow you for the ride and a $20. Or we can fuck for a hundred," she said.

I laughed. "Well, Ms. Hailey. I haven't fucked in over a year. I pretty much hung up my spurs."

She looked confused.

"I don't want a hand-job or a blowjob or to fuck. I've never paid for it, either."

She looked concerned, leaned away from me toward the passenger door. "I told you, I don't have money. If you're into some weird shit or got other ideas, you can let me out here..."

"Relax. I don't want anything from you but your story. I just want to talk. Besides, even if I did want to fuck, you're way too young for me. But you are a pretty girl."

Her shoulders loosened. She let out a sigh, patted the dog's head and stroked his ears. "Alright, then. Shit, man, you had me scared there for a minute. Most guys who give me rides want a blowjob or to fuck. A few broke-ass guys take the handy then try to talk their way into a free blowy or fuck. I pretty much stick to my guns unless the guy is hot or has drugs for trade. What do you want to talk about?" she asked.

"Well, how about telling me where you're from and how you ended up trading sex for rides and drugs. Then maybe you can tell me about the scariest or weirdest thing that's happened to you out here on America's great highways," I answered.

"Where you and your daughter from? What's her name, anyway?" she asked.

"Her name is Kristen and we're from San Diego. I live in the mountains. She lives in some hipster area called North Park."

"You two close?" she asked.

I cringed. *Fuck.* "Um... We fight a lot. It's mostly my fault. Her mom died right after she was born. Breast cancer. I was young and drinking way too much and left her with my sister for the first couple years of her life. I was pretty much off the rails. She still resents me for it. Now we fight over stupid shit."

She shook her head. "You came back into her life though, right?"

"Sure. I was around. My sister stayed involved. I got mostly sober. But I...uh... I had a job back then that required travel. I guess I wasn't around as much as I should have been."

"Shit. Better than my old man. Bastard went to prison when I was five and I haven't seen or heard from him since."

"Damn. Your mom raised you?" I asked.

"Shit. If you can call it that. She was too busy trying to find another man to support us. Fucked half the guys in Sandy. And those guys spent most of the time trying to fuck me. She finally got jealous and kicked my ass out when I was 17."

What the fuck do I say to that? "Sandy?" I finally asked.

"Oregon."

We were silent for a bit.

"You ever want to settle down?" I asked.

She looked out the passenger window for a beat, watching the desert flash by. "Well, I don't want to do this forever. I like meeting people and seeing the country. But, yeah, I'm hoping to land someplace, find a job or something. Maybe find a boyfriend, get an apartment or trailer to live in."

"Ever had a job?" I asked.

"Yeah. I worked at Subway back home. I worked two winters dancing in strip clubs. One in Denver, the other one was in Missoula."

"Why did you leave? Isn't dancing more stable than being on the road?"

"You'd think it would be. But things get shady quick in clubs. Some are just fronts for whorehouses; I didn't want some pimp running my life. In the legit ones, the cops or the owner or bouncer is always trying to get over on you. You know, take a cut, get you to fuck them or their buddies for free... I got slapped around more than a couple times."

We drove on in silence for a while. I thought about what she said about her old man being absent. I cringed thinking what might have become of my daughter, Kristen, when I took off the first time, when she was five. If my sister, Misty, didn't step in as a stable influence with a job and prospects...

Shit could have gone south quick. I was fucking lucky.

Since she seemed done talking, I turned on my driving soundtrack, mostly a bunch of sad, slow alt-country songs.

The girl rested her head on the window, closed her eyes, and snuggled the puppy. I looked over at her and wondered if she was really 22. She seemed young, but her cheap make-up made her look older and sleazy.

"Hey, can you put on something else? These sad songs are putting me to sleep," she said.

I switched to my '90s grunge playlist. It dawned on me that her falling asleep could be fatal in her line of work—at least until that puppy was grown.

"Thanks, man," she said. She turned her attention back to the desolate landscape rolling by.

I wanted to help her. But how? It would take a lot to get her out of this downward spiral she was on—social workers, a GED, probably rehab. She'd certainly needed therapy.

I decided the best I could do was give her a hundred bucks when I dropped her off. I figured it would go up her nose, but I didn't give a shit. It was one less old man she needed to fuck, one less roll of the dice that might end with some dude who got off to killing girls like her. And hell, I could certainly use the karma.

"Hey, can I charge my phone?" she asked.

"Yeah, no problem," I said.

She disconnected my phone and plugged hers in. She started texting someone right away.

Watching her, I could only think of my daughter. *Jesus, these kids always have their head down, eyes glued to the damn screen.*

She looked up about 25 minutes outside of Bakersfield. I figured I'd still get to Bishop before dark.

"Hey where the fuck are we?" She seemed concerned, maybe annoyed with herself for not paying attention to where I was taking her.

"I decided to drop you off in Bakersfield. It's not too far out of my way. See, sign right ahead: **Bakersfield 40 miles**." In truth, it would add over a hundred miles and 90 minutes or more to my trip. What the hell.

"Wow. Thanks, man. You sure I can't give you a freebie?"

We both laughed.

"I'm good. But how about you tell me your strangest or scariest story from the road. We got at least a half-hour before we get to Bako."

"Scary... Shit. I don't even know where to start. One time, I had to jump out of a moving semi. This trucker offered me a ride and a hundred for a fuck. We were still in the parking lot of a

Stuckey's. But the second he started driving, he pulled a coil of rope out. Started talking about how he was going to hogtie me, fuck me, and leave me on the side of the road, naked for other truckers who might enjoy a free piece. Scared the shit out of me."

"Jesus. Glad you got out. Did you get hurt? Did he stop?"

"Nah. I got a few scrapes. Fucker just drove away. I warned the other girl working the lot."

"Okay... How about weird?"

"That's easy. Two weeks ago, I was outside of Moab, Utah. I hitched a ride with these two Mormon missionary dudes heading to L.A.... They wore those shitty white shirts and cheap polyester black pants, had those skinny ties, two bikes on the roof rack. I figured they were about as safe a bet as I'd ever find. Thought to myself, I won't even need to put out. So, we got to talking and I could see these guys giving each other the look... You know, trying to figure out who was going to ask me the big ask... Then, I think, *Shit, these fuckers either want a three-way or are going to start preaching.* But you know what they wanted?"

"No idea," I answered.

"They wanted to stick it in my pussy and lay there. Said it was called soaking or some shit. No moving. Just let it sit in my pussy for a minute or two. They both wanted a turn. Didn't want me to move or take off my shirt, they didn't want to cum. Said it wasn't a sin to do that. Twisted motherfuckers."

I laughed. Twisted, indeed. "So, what did you do?"

"I told them, 'If you put it in, you pay up.' It would be $100 each. I told them half the old fuckers I screw can't cum. Hell, I'd go broke letting dudes put in for a minute or two for free. So, I said I'd give them both a handy to cover the gas and ride."

"What happened?"

"They told me they didn't have the money and they couldn't take a handy because it was a sin. Said to forget it... Then they started preaching at me. Fuckers. I made them drop me at the first rest stop. I don't want to hear that shit. The religious ones scare me."

Jesus, what a life. I got to call Kristen and make this shit better.

At a Wendy's near a gas stop outside of Bako, I dropped off the girl. She teared up when I gave her the hundred bucks, told her to get the dog and herself some food.

As I drove off, she waved.

In my rearview mirror, I watched her and Buster cross the overpass. Then head into the parking lot of the truck stop on the other side.

Author Bio

Twitter: @JDClappWrites   *Instagram:* @JDClapp

JD Clapp, based in San Diego, California, has pieces that appear in *Bristol Noir, Roi Fainéant Press, trampset, Punk Noir Magazine* and numerous other journals. He is a two-time Pushcart Prize nominee (non-fiction) and a three-time Best of the Net nominee (fiction and poetry). He is also a regular contributor to Poverty House.

Clapp dabbles in poetry with a couple chapbooks and creative nonfiction with a gritty slant. He is known for writing about addiction, photography, and hybrid works. In 2025, he has *Poachers and Pills* slated for publication with Cowboy Jamboree Press. He also has a second story collection, *A Good Man Goes South*, out through Anxiety Press.

Will-O-The-Wisp

By Aaron Paul Schaut

An angry buzz let Willow know it was time to remove the peanut butter cookies from the oven. Jean and John sat at a small, yellow Formica table, coloring and waiting for Grandma's warm, fork-pressed treats. "Grandma's cookies are the best," they said.

It's pretty steady that Willow watched the kids two or three times a week while her daughter, Sarah, ran errands or tended to other responsibilities. The joy of being a grandmother radiated from those cookies and her face as she made them.

Sarah and her husband Don did okay with him slinging cars at the Oldsmobile dealership. It kept the Stonebrook family swimming in their big kidney-shaped pool. He sold two brand-spankin' new Oldsmobile Toronados just last week.

Willow didn't have a pool, but her deceased husband did install a rather elaborate bomb shelter, diminishing any savings, a few years prior. That was 1963.

Now 1966, a year wrought with questions, Willow retrieved the mail after Sarah picked up the kids. There it was, big and bold on the cover of *Time Magazine*: **Is God Dead?**

Willow rolled her eyes in typical Willow fashion. She had no desire for such philosophical nonsense. Even in her late sixties, Willow was a city girl, more concerned with her modern scarfs and oversized Jackie O. sunglasses than any of that perverse Communist propaganda.

JFK died the same year as Willow's husband. According to Willow, both men were patriots of freedom. *There is most certainly a God*, she thought, *it's through Him that we carry on after such things. There better be a Hell—anyway—for Hitler and all those Communists.*

Willow carried with her a disdain for Communism since she was a little girl. This was only emphasized by the Red Scare of the '40s and '50s. Willow had no room in her life for anyone or anything resembling a Communist: the Hollywood Ten, Lester Cole, Chaplin. Now, there were beatniks and hippies. Her hatred, originating in Germany, validated by McCarthy and extended by the death of JFK, burned through her entire being.

Willow retreated to her bedroom, magazine in hand, staring at the family photos framed atop the tallboy dresser—her mirror above it. Her eyes lost focus in her reflection, the mirror became distorted and concave. A transformation had begun.

The woman in the mirror became younger, more beautiful. Her face flushed as she removed her scarf, a silken pastel floral print. She softly moved her fingertips around the reflection of a neck devoid of aging. She put her fingers to her lips before moving toward the dresser.

She slid the third drawer open, revealing garments of enticement—the kind you might wear on your wedding night or a night working a corner.

She slid off her Jackie-O. attire.

She took her time as dusk turned its dark blanket over the scene.

Clothing completely removed, she'd run her fingers along her soft skin, shivering through senses dormant during the day's light—The only melancholy was during that holy time when that mirror worked its magic. "There most certainly is a Hell and most certainly is a God," she whispered while sliding a silky black negligée over her now long blonde hair, around her perfectly defined shoulders, and over supple breasts budding at attention. Arousal was embodied in each goosebump, warm as it might be.

She applied red lipstick, the color you thought of when imagining sex. That deep and rich red Marilyn wore as she slid across the screen.

Willow blotted her lips on a square of handkerchief embossed with the initials of her late husband—sensitive to the sentimentality of the moment. She added high heels and a raincoat and was written as a vision of perfect allurement, so it was told, or shown, by her reflection in that mirror.

Willow ambled along the sidewalk freshly cleansed by a soft rain, the full moon highlighting the accents of all the things around her. She walked to The Elbow Room, just blocks from her house. A dim glow and the energy of movement shone through the pub's windows, shared by moonlight and wetness, and it all gave the place the look of an Edward Hopper or Norman Rockwell painting.

She set herself on a barstool and ordered red wine.

Her beauty and sex appeal were not missed by Joe, the bartender, as he handed her the glass "on the house."

Near the entryway, in a booth curved and upholstered, three boys sat. They had the bouncing legs, appearance, and energy of the times. One brunet in a mod jacket, one ginger in a white T-shirt, and another brunet with a collared shirt. The three talked about Ezra Pound and a little bit of Vonnegut. They stood or sat and moved and talked with their hands. They played music on the jukebox that shook the place with intense, wild rhythms and the dark lyrics you might expect when on the verge of war, or "post-war," or however one felt at 21 in 1966.

Willow, though maintaining her façade, felt disgusted by their presence. To her, their Nietzsche, their Pound, and their lack of proper attire for a night out were all red flags. Communist red. Though the boys were just boys, embracing their rebellious age, caught up in the beats, Willow would never see it this way.

To her, they were a threat who reeked of their parents' money. Those kinds of kids always had loads of their parents' money and that would make the score even sweeter. She wouldn't have concerned herself with money had her husband not been forced to pour their savings into that bomb shelter. Another result of the Reds.

She led with her leg and faced the boys. "Are you boys going to just talk all night, or are you going to do something about it?"

The boys lit up as though Sinatra was taking the stage at the Sands. No amount of church, war, or Nietzsche could muffle hot-blooded desire at their age.

So, the one with the mod-looking coat said to Willow, "What would you like us to do?"

"How about you buy me another glass of wine?" she replied, as cool as Mary Tyler Moore on the *Dick Van Dyke Show*.

And the boys stumbled over each other in a race to order that drink.

"So, tell me, baby, how come I haven't seen you around here before? I would most certainly have noticed an angel such as yourself dropping into a place such as this."

The other two boys pressed to get closer.

"Maybe you're not as keen as you think," Willow said as the wineglass licked the red from her lips. She pulled the brunet in and kissed him deeply before pushing him back, shouting, "Who's going to ask me to dance?" and, oh boy, were those boys ready to dance.

She strutted to the jukebox and asked for a dime, which each boy suddenly had in hand.

She played a seductive "eeny-meeny" with them before slowly—sensually—taking the coin from the nearest boy and sliding it into the Wurlitzer coin slot.

Cliff Richard and the Drifters' "High Class Baby" pounded the room. The four shook and grooved and they petted each other while others looked on.

"Life ain't always wasted on the youth," shouted Old Man Willie Wilder from the brass rail of the bar, toward Joe the bartender, and then they both took a drink.

"Boys, whatta ya say we find somewhere a little more comfortable to take this little party of ours?" Willow's question pierced through the music and lit each boy on fire.

"You bet!" "Let's ditch this place!" "Groovy!"

"How much?" asked the mod—keener than the others.

"Awe, honey, how much do you think I'm worth?"

"You can take whatever I got," said the ginger with an ear-to-ear grin. His freckles would have jumped off of his face if they could.

"I'll take whatever you got and then some, boys."

One of the boys put the back of his hand to his forehead, pretending to faint and swoon.

Willow rubbed her index and middle fingers against her thumb, acknowledging her worth. Her husband's passing had left her with little cushion for day-to-day errands, much less societal weapons. She'd take their money, and then some.

"Okay, then!" The three boys, eager to spend, pranced and bounced and jumped around while following Willow's far more graceful lead.

"Right this way, boys." She led them along the drive and up around the house.

"Groovy place! Where are you taking us? You got a back patio or pool?"

"It's all a surprise."

"Far out!"

Willow opened the heavy door of the shelter—its weak, flickering light shining up the cement stairway. She took the hand of the boy nearest and led him down while the other two followed. The second boy burst past to inspect the small Regency radio that sat up on a small bookshelf. He began tuning into whatever rock-'n'-roll he could find.

Willow lit some candles and a cigarette.

This was no "little shelter." Sure, there was a pantry loaded with canned goods and preserves, but there was also a small bed, a chrome table with two red chairs, a very small kitchenette with various liquors, and still enough room to groove.

"Quite the little love nest you have here, lady. Does taking us here keep your man ignorant of your side hustle?"

"Guess what I have?" Willow asked while making drinks.

"Oh, boy! Please don't leave us hanging!"

Willow reached into a cupboard and pulled out a small canister.

The boys had the look of children waiting for fireworks to go off.

She opened the tin and waved it around, showing the boys its contents. "Freshly baked peanut butter cookies! Let's just say they were my grandmother's recipe. Go ahead, take one." She smiled, her grandmotherly smile evident even through her young features.

One of the boys reached for the can.

"*Uh-uh-uh.*" She waved her finger back and forth in front of his face. "Cough it up, boys."

The three boys emptied their pockets onto the small table. "Will this work?" one asked.

Willow picked up the money and counted it. "This will do just fine."

"Lady, will you marry me?" one of the boys said while chewing. Crumbs were falling all over him and the floor.

Willow flirtatiously smiled while another boy stood near the pantry, touching random things and saying, "Man... What a relic!"

Willow sat on the bed with the tin of cookies. "If you're looking to touch something..." She slid her overcoat down and around her, onto the mattress, her skin glowing and her breasts exposed through the black, semi-sheer lingerie.

Two of the boys looked on while the one with the mod jacket quickly slid next to her.

She kissed him a little.

He kissed her a lot.

"Are the two of you just going to stand there?" Willow asked with a look of lust.

"Ma'am...?" one said while the other just stood, looking.

"Don't you boys want another cookie?"

"I mean, yes, ma'am. I would love another."

"You're going to have to earn it, aren't you, dear? Only good little boys who finish all of Grandma's supper get more dessert." Willow winked. "I'm not tryin' to be a square, but I do believe those are the rules."

"Lady, looking like you do, you can make up any rules you like," said the ginger. He slid around the side of her and began kissing her shoulder.

Willow put her hand through his locks. "That's a good boy. Are you a good boy?"

He nodded a little while the first boy continued to kiss Willow's lips and neck.

There were crumbs on her skin and falling onto the bed linens.

The brunet with the collared shirt couldn't take it anymore and slid up and around on the bed.

Willow put one hand over the bulge in his slacks and her other hand on another's. Her youthful desires were every bit as strong as theirs; she was wet as they were erect. She slipped off the first boy's corduroy slacks after pushing him to stand up, then she began to suck.

The other boys clumsily undressed while kissing and lapping at her.

She lay down and let all three have their way with her, and each other, while Elvis Presley's "Puppet on a String" filled the room.

While Elvis offered "truest love" and begged and pleaded through his words, moaning filled the room, blending in with Elvis's background singers, in an off-key sort of devil chant.

The boys came all over that bomb shelter, all those explosions on the wrong side of the walls. Willow came too, vigorously and with intent. The song slowly finished out.

She stood up and lit a cigarette while the boys lay strung out over the little bed.

Willow reached past the little pile of money and then into a small drawer in the hutch.

Turning, she held in her hand a .38 that belonged to her father. Slick and long-nosed, a WWII officer's firearm.

The boys slid back. "Woah, lady!"

"96 Tears" blasted out of the small radio.

The ginger boy yelled, so she shot him in the forehead.

"Too many teardrops," the lyrics teased.

The other two yelped while looking at each other with big, wide eyes—covered in spatters of their friend's blood and brains.

"Cry, cry, cry," the lyrics bounced off the walls and blended with screams.

The redhead's cash flew out of his hand, spilled onto the mattress and floor.

"96 Tears," an organ melody. Sardonic anthem of violence and retribution. A circus melody for this three-man circus.

"Eat another goddamn cookie!" Willow yelled while the two cowered against the cement wall.

"My God!" the mod yelled, naked, tears in his eyes, as his friend speechlessly shivered next to him.

"Do you honestly think God gives a good goddamn about you kids? You walk around, smiling and dancing and preaching all that bullshit around town, like you know the first goddamn thing about anything. Listen for once. I said...eat the god-damn cookies!"

Through the speakers came the familiar voice of Wolfman Jack singing about mercy.

Willow's demeanor was becoming more angry, more violent, with each look from the boys. The Stones distorted guitar intro blended into the scene. She inched forward and shoved a cookie in the mod boy's mouth.

The crumbs combined with his tears, his buddy's blood, and all that brain.

She put the barrel of the gun to his head and pulled his mouth up into her cunt. All the while, she cackled the kind of laugh reserved for the insane, the sinister look of those mob mugshot smiles in the papers. She pressed his lips hard against hers and fiercely swiveled his head up and down.

She moaned and laughed and came while the boy cried out a muffled scream, "Satisfaction" still whirling around the room.

The other boy flinched as Willow convulsed.

She shot twice into his chest—the mod boy still firmly pressed between her thighs.

He pushed back hard but immediately felt that steel barrel on his face. "You crazy fucking bitch!" he shouted, fluids of all kinds—cookie crumbs and all—mixing together on his face.

Willow backed away, gun still pointed at him. She used her other hand to pull a cigarette from the pack and lit it with her husband's Zippo. She loved the feeling of it all.

She loved the violence of the rape and the reins in her hands.

She began telling a story. "You see, boy? It was 1921. I was taken, you know, about your age, the very age you see me now. I was taken by Communist soldiers in a Berlin alleyway. You know what I was doing? I was taking my grandmother's cookies to my father, who was stitching soles onto soldiers' boots." Her insane look had become one of desperate sadness. "Some of the boots had been worn by soldiers who lost their souls to the war. I was just a young woman with a tin of cookies, minding her business."

"I... I don't... Please, God, let me go!"

"After the soldiers were done, they stood over me, eating the cookies. They laughed, while cookie crumbs fell with their spit onto my face... and cum covered my bare skin!" She was practically foaming at the mouth.

"Lady, I'm s-s-s-sorry—"

"Stop! I am not finished with my story. You see? I never told anyone about what happened, but it changed me—"

"—Please..."

"Eat the last one."

She handed him the cookie, but he didn't take it.

"I said, eat it!"

She threw it at his face.

He threw himself back, hitting his head against the wall.

Willow put her cigarette out on his face.

It sizzled in his tears and the blood and brain and cum.

"Pathetic," she said before raising the gun to his face— pulling the trigger.

His Commie-red blood and pinko brains pooled with his friends', and it was all sprinkled with those cookie crumbs.

Like a Pollack Painting, she thought. "Pollack was also a Communist sympathizer." She was talking to the boys as though they could hear her. "This is a perfect portrait of your kind of scum." Maybe the boys could hear her from the Hell she assumed would house their red-tinted souls.

She turned off the radio, took the bottle of wine and the cash, and walked up the cement stairway. After opening the hatch, she turned and spit into the now-dark cavern.

The morning had broken and found Sarah approaching her mother, who was standing, staring at herself in that bedroom mirror, still in that lingerie and those heels. Bright red lipstick on her lips, although fading. An empty bottle of wine and some cash atop the dresser.

Willow was shaking and staring at herself—her aged features had returned.

"Mom, what in God's name are you doing? We have to get a move on. We have church this morning and Don is finally going to fill in that dreadful old bomb shelter Dad built. Why aren't you dressed? What are you wearing?"

Willow looked through Sarah, while Sarah looked at her mom with so much concern, as only a daughter could have.

"Mom!"

"Dear?" Willow spoke softly. She was lost in her old age but well aware of the past. Every time she looked in that mirror, she was given another chance to defend freedom and make a little money while she did it. The embodiment of Capitalism, the essence of patriotism.

"Mom let's get you ready for church. Why on earth is everything covered in cookie crumbs? What is this all over you? Is this blood?"

Willow slowly pointed to herself in the mirror. She didn't have the words. She'd lost the words but knew she needed to keep her family shielded from what she truly was.

Sarah took her mom's hand and began helping her get cleaned up.

Don, outside with the kids, was waiting for the cement truck to arrive.

Sarah dressed her mom in her Sunday best, as beautiful as Jackie Kennedy, then walked her out of the house.

After getting her mom situated in the Oldsmobile, Sarah went to Don. "Honey, after you're done filling this awful thing, could you do me one more favor?"

"Anything, honey."

"Don, I'd like you to take all of the mirrors out of the house—It's time."

Author Bio

Site: AaronSchaut.com   Instagram: @AaronPaulSchaut

Aaron Paul Schaut is known for his heartfelt and relatable stories told without judgment. Born in Escanaba and now living in Grand Rapids, Michigan, he draws inspiration from his diverse experiences. His series, These Americans, explores themes of escape and belonging, while his novellas *Bricks* and *Lucid America* continue this journey.

Schaut wrote the short story "The Depression of John Stonebrook," featured in *Starlite Pulp Review #3* alongside modern fiction greats like Craig Clevenger and Manny Torres. When not writing, Schaut works with his band Dynaflo, enjoys riding his motorcycle, and spends time with the many animals of Michele's Rescue.

More From Our Authors

Gus is lost and found—and lost again. He seeks blurry fragments of his identity in shit-hole bars and girls who never stay. Like Tina, he thought time would wash her away, but some memories are tattoos—deeply rooted marks that never fade. Somewhere between coffee-stained notebooks and jukebox melodies, he's haunted by what could've been. Set in the hazy gray of '90s Michigan, *Lover's Rock* is a story of chasing an identity and girl who left a scar he can't erase.

Lover's Rock by Aaron Paul Schaut is a literary duet with *Counting Crows* by Neda Aria. These stories follow Gus and Tina through the echoes of a past they can't outrun. These books cum together even though they are distant and apart. The experience is a books/reader ménage à trois.

LEWDS

By Slxt Vxmit

Living is hard, no matter your lifestyle. With a 9 to 5, 5 to 9, or 24/7 job or persona, it's easy to feel collared by everyone watching you. The stress to keep surviving. Stay clean or dry-eyed or even mildly amused.

That's why I try to make my life sing. Being a metal and emo fan, it's no surprise my journey involves a lot of screaming or lashing out at myself or others. But that's the color of life (even if it's mostly black) and mirroring that is how I model myself. Rainbow blotches in my hair, neon Demonia boots, glow-in-the-dark gauges. But then the softness of otaku hoodies, lash filters, and an online aesthetic that glitters like a pretty in punk MySpace page.

Gotta make myself happy, invest in myself to keep afloat financially or otherwise. Even when I wake up to mean messages about my "pincushion face," I gotta keep going. Swallow the bitterness like a shot of Fireball, let the burn in my slim stomach propel me. Wipe the sleep from my eyes and remind myself at least this means I can stay home, control my destiny with a video camera, keep social the way I want. Which means blocking the ranting randos who come raid my Facebook pages or wherever, looking to troll, to spectate or gawk after knowing them as bullies in school or co-workers at kitchens from what seems like past lives.

Lots of people would be surprised to know plenty of sex workers are introverted or asexual the other 95% of their day. They compartmentalize their e-bait advertising for the freedom of a flexible or even anti-social schedule, or join the randy ranks of cam modeling mistakenly thinking they'll roll in dough easy peasy lemon squeezy. But it's with a bit of a sigh I have to admit the "work" half holds its weight as much as the "sex" part in the phrase "sex work."

So, time to clock in.

I shower, straighten my hair, apply neon-edged makeup and spend about an hour in the steamy bathroom just trying to take the best "candid" pix in a towel to play peekaboo with. Then I edit the snaps in devilish filters and screamo fonts with my username so I have sets for censored advertising and ones for paid subscribers. It takes half as long to convince myself everything is at its prime. When you spend a career thinking of your looks as a commodity, it's like pruning a tree: always a little more that feels like it needs snipping or angling to be proportional or eye-catching enough.

Flipping through an unusable gallery of accidental blinks and awkward smiles becomes extra frustrating. Time wasted. Minutes murdered that could've made money already. If I stew long enough, I get a pang for the confidence I had on coke. But then I remember that's also just another sump of sums. A cycle that wobbles out of control like a tire hovering off the hub.

To distract myself, I post my best censored shot on X and share some shitposty memes. It may seem silly to crossover worlds with comedy and sex, but it's what makes me stand out. Buyers to gauge my personality and make it easier to interact with me, reach a larger audience in general like I've been doing since I got internet access. Hell, maybe they'll even see some show or movie I'm into and request a cosplay. Maybe they'll think of me more like some unrequited crush they had. Reachable, relatable. Worth paying the rent for.

Plus, it's not just for the gooners. It's how I stay sane and entertained and how I make other sex work friends. Speaking of blurring worlds, I plan on doing that by streaming a sexy *Guitar Hero* Let's Play today. Maybe I'll strum some Blur in a lace bikini while simps reimburse my vodka soda fund.

After five years of this grind, gotta keep things fresh. Keep suckering the sissy boys into buying humiliating voice memos. Keep up on the acronyms they request related to cock and ball torture and dick ratings. Keep meeting goals to get these bills taken care of, the kitties fed.

I stretch and decide I need some fuel in me too, especially to buffer my stomach lining for the impending drink stream. As I tend to my tabby cat, petting her with one hand, I text in the other. Reel in a buyer to Apple Pay for a breakfast delivery—not just for me, but to supply the kibbles to my comfort creature as well.

That's one goal down. A small satisfaction that makes me grin. Feel like fretting over financials last night wasn't so necessary. I can do this. *Have* been doing this, I remind myself. Can turn just my genetic gifts my into groceries, pictures into providing for my family.

Yet I still have to respect my family in whatever form it comes in more traditional ways. To earn my keep, I do their dishes despite the sensory Hell it can be scrubbing away salsa and burnt bits from congealing plates: a whole leaning tower's worth while the leaky nozzle sprays me haphazardly, speckling my Slipknot jammies with God knows what. Oh, well. Being a seductress doesn't save you from stains or chores. And it certainly doesn't make you queen of the castle, so I have to retreat to my room and bar the door to get down to business.

Sound muffled by a million fuzzy pillows and psychedelic tapestries, my room is a blacklight delight. A cozy gamer cave. Changing into a cam outfit with lots of chokers but leaving little to the imagination, I plop onto a shaggy slime-green pillow. Knead its fur as I fight away "stage" jitters to go live with Jell-O shots. Strapped with the plastic guitar controller, I wave hello to curious Facebookers looking for a chill but scandalous show. I'm a soft-talker but my voice strengthens as chat shoots the shit with me. They request songs and challenge me to harder chords, making a drinking game out of my missed notes. They send tips and emojis as I engage with them.

O. Ur an OF chick, someone types. **Wat weird requests u get?**

"Oh, you know, the usual doozies," I laugh, trying to flicker my attention between the live chat and rocky Britpop.

C'mon. Spill the tea, a female friend insists. **Any adult babies? Scatsters?**

"Oh my gooosh," I groan, trying to shimmy and stretch my pinky far enough to hit the far bars on the guitar and recall the insane messages I get on the daily. "You have no idea. That's the baseline. I hope they're kidding sometimes... Kudos for knowing their fetish and getting what they want, I guess." I shrug and glance at my door, hoping no one home can hear me.

Some viewers spread puke emotes. Others, tears of laughter. As more people pour in my stream, it gets harder to keep up with their messages. Prioritize regulars and big spenders, catch up newbies to funnel them into checking out my harder core content.

I fail another song and have to take a couple more swigs, feeling looser. Opening up that some men request vids where I finger my bellybutton or pour wax into it to make molds they send away for. Decorated to be kinda like their own kinky Dragon Balls. "Sneezing is big. Guys wanna pause the video to see all the stills you look overwhelmed. Or arm pit fetishes are a thing, too. Some girls online will pixelate their photos so you can't get a free pic. They do that with feet, too. Some YouTubers do it as a joke but it's legit. I guess people think the crook between your arm can kinda look like a slit or feel nice and soft." I shrug like, *to each their own.*

Woooow, some type just before I hit Star Power on the song "Bleed It Out" that lights up my fretboard electric blue. I'm still a bit nervous a roommate could barge in and ruin my shot over some little question, so I talk faster. Also, to get to as many commenters ASAP.

Some of my SW "contemporaries" join the chat, complaining that the worst part is when those freaky subs have the gall to lowball or flake on us.

I have to agree, things can get awkward when there's rejection on either side. Like when I refuse to do any age-play scenarios. Some dudes get stalkery over it—not to me, but I've seen it four times over, the cyberstalking and relentless trash-talking. But when it truly comes to my most outlandish offer received: someone requesting I get revenge on their behalf. Like totaling somebody's car.

"Imagine," I ask the chat. "Little ol' me flying out to some horny whacko just to jump on their enemy's shitty Honda?" I shake my head. "They'd probably want me to meet them for piss play after at a hotel. You never know who you're engaging with."

You can engage w/ me, someone winks in chat and suggests a multiplayer battle over a hit Silverchair single.

From my knees on a fuzzy plush body pillow, I strum my acceptance. Things are getting comfier with support and from the crowd. It's like I've got a virtual audience in addition to the rockabilly one moshing on my screen.

They ask about what buyers and bands and bondage I prefer. Some even hit me up about the other ventures on my page, like how I sell Kandi bead jewelry and splatter paintings. They just want something I was a part of and touched. Something a li'l colorful and ravey like me.

Lemme Barbara Walters u, someone with a reporter emoji insists. **Wat has this lifestyle taught u, hmmm?**

I laugh and think about it as I hum and riff. "Um, well, there's this whole new spicy vocabulary. Finding out dick rate pictures are in. CBT: cock and ball torture. SPH: small penis humiliation. Sometimes I have to research terms on Urban Dictionary or FetLife... Oh my gosh, and the spend money to make money concept. There's a multitude of props, seasonal outfits, expensive makeup to boost the content and likes... I mean, who would ever think one day I'd need to invest in a strap-on as a business expense?"

Pumped up on payouts, playlists, and Monster Dreamsicle, I keep answering questions and doing little dances for tips and reacts that charge the algorithm. I'm really having a good time listening to the music recs and *Guitar Hero* tricks, interacting with classic, new, and potential connects, when my Facebook feed gets cut with a copyright strike. Right before I play "Misery Business." How's that for irony?

Oh, well.

When you're making content, things can always go wrong. Murphy's Law and all that shit. Sometimes scenes can go funny or embarrassing like with awkward sounds or angles, so at least I have nothing to be ashamed of here. No real setbacks when the money is earned through messages and Marketplace merch. No nip or lip slips to earn a ban. No reports by jealous puritans.

All in all, a fun new experience. Good days are how I remember to keep pushing.

I'm very lucky to be where I am. Lounging in the comfort of my chill cave, making conversation and coin off of other weirdos. Having unconventional platforms like FB, X, Insta, Telegram, Kik, Whatsapp, Snapchat, Discord, BlueSky, et cetera. Knowing I have options beyond OnlyFans, like Fansly that takes less percentage cuts, doesn't have as many unexplainable bannings (who knew other places would restrict the words choke, jail, bukkake, drinking, or paddling), withheld or lagging payments. Not as many scammers demanding chargebacks on received customs.

I feel supported not just by my real fans who stick with me across sites, but by companies like Fansly who stand by their backbone of SWs. Other sites like OF, on the other hand, try too often to underplay its base of lewd creators, wanting to rebrand like Patreon with exclusive podcasts or cooking shows. When the market exploded around Covid with so many people stuck in their houses, horny and/or poor, celebrities like Bella Thorne tried to get on board for a cash grab—but then would back out before launch, sending credit card processors scrambling after a million refunds. Everybody got scared by the seedy association.

Add this to sites inflating their "top X.XX% of creators" badges by including buyer accounts who will never post anything, and obviously I want something less volatile. A cut from a brand where girls don't mostly make McDonald's money.

I make a killing by no means, but I get by, and that's what matters most. No more sad times like grade school, where I'd be stuck wearing Great Value threads to hide how I feel inside. To get picked on for being too poor and plain or out of fashion. I wouldn't say I don't still get called ugly or a pinhead for my alternative appearance, but there's obviously quantifiable proof there are many more who like me.

All the bully barbs are basically a compliment or motivation, wish fulfillment. So what if I'm less approachable to the preachy, judgey people? I'll find my fans and even people to be funny and familiars with in the meantime.

My flame will still burn on.

I know it will.

AuthOr BiO

Facebook.com/Jaida.Fronzak   Twitter: @SlxtVxmit

Instagram: @MorgueBabii   Telegram: @SlxtVxmit

Slxt Vxmit is the real girl who inspired this short story series! She is available on social media for custom vid/pic requests and on Fansly (/SlxtVxmit) for a standard nude subscription. She is also selling kandi bead jewelry, colorful paintings, and her DropBox bundle with over 1000 lewd pictures and videos.

Additionally, show your financial support for her on Cash App $slxtVxmit and Venmo @SlxtVxmit

Thanks for reading! Find more transgressive fiction (poems, novel(la)s, anthologies) at: Outcast-Press.com

Twitter, TikTok & Instagram: @OutcastPress

Facebook.com/OutcastPress1

E-mail proof of your Amazon/Goodreads review to OutcastPress@gmail.com & we'll mail you free stickers/bookmarks!